UNLIKELY
ALLIES

Unlikely Allies

Published by The Conrad Press in the United Kingdom 2019

Tel: +44(0)1227 472 874
www.theconradpress.com
info@theconradpress.com

ISBN 978-1-911546-72-6

Illustrations by Maria Priestley.
Typesetting by Charlotte Mouncey, www.bookstyle.co.uk
The Conrad Press logo was designed by Maria Priestley.

Printed and bound in Great Britain
by Clays Ltd, Elcograf S.p.A.

Other books in the Battle of the Roses series by
Davina Jolley

Book One:

Primrose

For Janice Blake
14.07.60 – 29.12.18
Everyone needs at least one good friend,
Jan was mine.

UNLIKELY ALLIES

THE SECOND BOOK OF THE BATTLE OF THE ROSES

DAVINA JOLLEY

ILLUSTRATIONS BY MARIA PRIESTLEY

CONTENTS

1. A DISCOVERY

On the Isle of Rosa, Primrose was making good on her escape by using one of the many rivers that wove their way through the Ancient Forest. She was hopelessly lost and realised that pinning all of her hopes on a legend she had heard the night before, from otters of all things, was more than a little bit absurd. She would have laughed at anyone else who thought such a thing could be true, but Primrose was desperate.

She still used the river to mask her trail, and it was not easy. She was having a lot of difficulty in keeping her balance and her temper, but she knew it was important to keep both, especially if she was ever to find the Ancient Tree that the otters had spoken of.

Primrose was relieved at how quiet the forest appeared as she made her way awkwardly upriver. Her eyes darted side-to-side as she tried hard not to be spotted, but there were so many hiding places within the rocks and the undergrowth that adorned the river bank. However, she refused to let her guard down or leave a trail for Victor, the tiresome hare, that had persistently followed her for the last two days. Seeing no animals in the forest was strange in itself, but she knew from experience that she could not take their absence for granted.

Her newly gained freedom was far too important to her, just as much as her search for the Ancient Tree.

There were times when Primrose felt sorry for the damage she had left behind. She had not meant to hurt Briony, Elina or the wolf cubs, but each time her heavy, stone foot sunk into the soft mud or made her stumble painfully the guilt lessened. Being turned into a statue and left that way for years had definitely, in her opinion, been an awful over-reaction to her losing her temper thirteen years ago! Briony should not have done it! It was cruel and unfair. Primrose felt a tear begin to trace its way down her cheek, she rubbed at it angrily, smudging the filth that encrusted her face. She was annoyed with herself as she realised she had started to cry again.

If only Primrose had remained patient, then she would have had two perfectly formed feet, but no, Primrose had acted the way she always did; rashly and impulsively. She had not given Elina's magic enough time to complete the transformation, from statue to human. Well, it was too late now, Primrose thought angrily. She just had to accept the fact she was lumbered with the stone foot for the rest of her life!

When Primrose had climbed into the hole next to the river, she hadn't known it was also a temporary refuge for an otter family. Even she would have given that hole a wide berth. No one in their right mind would think sharing a hole with two adult otters rearing three young kits was a good idea. The hole, though, had proved to be a safe place for Primrose. The otters had not discovered her and Victor had not found her. Primrose had been very, very lucky.

Primrose hoped that Victor was now far away. She still couldn't believe how quiet the forest was and prayed that her luck would not run out. She feared her clumsy progress would be spotted by some kind of animal and then reported back to Jack, Briony's husband.

Primrose was very much aware that Jack would be searching for her soon, as well as all the other animals that she had upset in the past, and there were many of them! It was extremely important to her to keep her progress hidden.

Unknown to Primrose, the absence of the animals in the forest that day was because they had gathered for Briony's funeral, which would later be followed by a meeting at the fallen oak tree. Primrose was not even aware of the full extent of the damage she had left behind. She believed Briony had fainted from the shock of seeing her alive again.

Now, she wondered if she would ever find a safe place to stay. There were so many tall trees that overhung the river and the steep banks that they continually blocked her view. She began to think she might have to scramble up the steep banks and leave the safety of the river, fearing she may have missed the Ancient Tree altogether.

The otters had said the Ancient Tree was huge and that it pierced the sky, she was beginning to think they had exaggerated. Primrose realised what was huge to an animal was not necessarily huge to a human and her hope for a safe place to stay began to fade. According to the otter's legend, the Rose family had lived inside it once, but animals now feared it and considered it to be a place of Dark Magic. To Primrose it sounded like the perfect place to hide and figure out what to do with her life, but she couldn't help think that perhaps the otters had lied about that too.

Rounding a bend in the river, Primrose stopped. In front of her stood the Ancient Tree. It was unmistakeable, colossal and magnificent. She stared at the legendary tree, amazed at the sheer size of it. The otters had not lied!

The tree towered majestically above her. Its branches were easily several times the size of a normal tree. They stretched up, dominating the skyline. The view from those lofty spires must be truly amazing. Even the immense trunk could have fitted at least six cars inside of it. It wasn't hard to imagine that someone could have lived inside that enormous tree.

Awed by its magnificent size, Primrose quickly made her way across the river, heading towards the tangled root system. The mighty roots were just as huge as the branches and plunged solidly into the river bed and bank. As Primrose stepped through and into the cavernous root system, her breath was taken away at the immense space that surrounded her, even in the dim light; it was awe inspiring.

She believed that the maze of interlocking roots must have been created by the powerful wave the otters had spoken of as it had swept the riverbank away. The ancient roots circled her and gave her a feeling of comfort and protection. To others it would have felt like a terrible prison, but Primrose felt no uneasiness or anything sinister. In fact, it felt as though she had come home.

On the river bed, Primrose noticed small footprints and guessed them to be those of Victor, who had pursued her so valiantly. Now, new prints were added, human footsteps and great square blobs made by her stone foot. She watched those deeper prints slowly fill with water. Primrose smirked and wondered what an explorer would make of those prints, a new species maybe - a rhinogirl or a girlaphant!

Once more, she looked around. There needed to be a way into the Ancient Tree, but where? Primrose was determined to find it.

By the time Primrose had searched every root below and above eye level, her footprints on the river bed would easily give her position away, especially to Victor. Once more Primrose admired the persistence of her worthy adversary, but covering her tracks was not a priority at the moment. Primrose needed to find the way in.

Finally, she hauled herself onto the land and searched every inch of the trunk, looking for tell-tale signs of any crack that resembled a doorway or an indentation that could give away a footfall or a step for an entry higher up, but she found nothing.

Just like Victor, she could find no signs of a way in. She was convinced that the entrance would be at ground level, so she returned to the river bank, sat down and studied the root system and water level marks intently, still nothing. Tired of the continual struggle Primrose rested her head against the solid trunk, closed her eyes and wondered why her life had to be so difficult.

However, Primrose was determined not to give up; she was no quitter! She was not going to cry. She would try again. With a deep sigh, she opened her eyes; it was time for one more attempt. She told herself to be systematic, patient and to take it slowly.

Primrose knew that the river level back in the days when The Ancient Tree was a home would have been different to that of todays. Even the flood would have washed away the soil from under the roots. So, she tried looking at the different soil colours in the banks, hoping to find a clue. I'm a proper scientist now she thought with a smile, but the smile faded as she realised only one person had ever cared if she'd been good at anything, and that person, Briony, would never forgive her now, not after what she had done to Elina. Primrose, disheartened, still found nothing.

Feeling her temper start to flare, Primrose wanted to kick something hard and scream. She wanted to break something, hurt something, but she managed to rein her feelings in and maintain control. She took a deep breath, counted to ten and felt her heart start to beat slower. Eventually, she calmed down. She absently scratched her stone foot; it seemed to tingle.

She looked up and saw four pieces of rope dangling loosely. Could something have been tied to them, she wondered. They seemed to be incorrectly placed for a ladder, but perhaps they were meant to be pulled. Primrose galvanised herself into action: she needed to find out if pulling on the ropes would gain her access to the tree.

Climbing the roots was out of the question; her stone foot slipped as the roots became steeper and gave her no grip. She needed a hook. Searching along the river bank, she found a few suitable sticks and branches and hobbled back to the tree.

After countless tries, Primrose at last managed to hook one of the sticks through a loop in one of the ropes and pulled. The loop gave way, rotten with age and she collapsed onto her backside painfully. Primrose stayed where she was, amidst pieces of broken branches and sticks; they were a taunting reminder of her numerous, failed attempts. She was tired, hungry, thirsty and almost ready to give up. Her spirits sank.

Soon she would have to return to the otters' hole - it would be getting too dark to see anything clearly within an hour or two. She knew she had been lucky so far. Primrose became nervous, she still couldn't understand why the forest had been so quiet and devoid of animals that day. She looked around warily. Taking a deep breath, Primrose made a wish, 'If anyone ever loved me once, please show me a sign.'

Closing her eyes, she rested her head on her knees and tried to think what else she could possibly try? Surely she wasn't meant to live the rest of her life in a hole!

Her ears heard it first; faint scratchings, something was moving above her head. Her eyes had no trouble spotting the small rodent. She shuddered as she saw the rat. It was not one of her favourite animals and it was looking directly at her, staring her out, whiskers twitching and sitting on its hind legs. Primrose looked at the rat intently. It seemed strange to her that the rat wasn't the least bit scared of her. In fact, it seemed very curious and continued staring at her with its black, beady eyes. An inner voice seemed to urge her to throw something at it and scare it away.

It would have been so easy for Primrose to throw a stone or a branch at it and make it scuttle away, but she ignored the voice and sat watching it instead. She needed to make up her mind whether to leave, or make one final attempt to find an entry. Primrose absent-mindedly rubbed her stone foot again, it seemed to itch. She shrugged the feeling off and once more looked at the rat.

Finally, the brown rat seemed bored; it turned its black, beady eyes from her and scuttled away across the roots.

Two things happened; Primrose heard a creak and then saw

a small crack appear on the spot where the rat had stood. She sprang up, climbed precariously to the spot and found a small twig, or was it? Balancing awkwardly, Primrose pushed it one way, then another, nothing.

She pulled it. The twig thing moved, it actually moved! Primrose felt a growing excitement, butterflies fluttered in her stomach! Then she heard a wonderful noise, something cracked above her head. She pulled the twig further, and with a loud, dry creaking noise, an opening appeared and a staircase was lowered.

It didn't quite reach the river bed, but Primrose was able to reach it, just. She moved as quickly as possible, not wishing for the staircase to be retracted, and hauled herself onto the first tread. Steadying herself, she started to climb.

Just as she was about to put her stone foot inside the Ancient Tree, a sudden, frightening noise made her jump violently and she nearly lost her already precarious balance.

A whooshing noise sounded all around her, as powerful jets of water were released from each tree root and washed away every print, every stick and every branch. Primrose's trail was completely obliterated. Primrose smiled with relief.

Nervously, she entered the Ancient Tree. The staircase closed behind her with a sudden, loud snap, making her jump again.

Plunged into sudden darkness, Primrose realised she was sealed inside and sunk to her knees. She could see nothing, hear nothing and feel nothing. She knew she was trapped again, but strangely she still didn't feel frightened.

Resigned to her fate, she sat down and tried to look at things positively. She was out of the river, the place was warm and dry and although it was dark, she felt safe. She sat down, drew her knees up to her chest and waited for her eyes to adjust to the lack of light.

Primrose was becoming an expert at waiting. All she needed now was a little bit of patience.

2. OWL'S LAST REPORT

With the tallest tree in the Ancient Forest within the owl's sights, the bird tucked its wings back and glided smoothly towards it and then through its entrance hole. The owl landed perfectly on a silver perch without making a sound. It was the first time the owl had returned without a summons. The Summoner had told it previously to report back after the meeting at the fallen oak tree, and that's precisely what it had done. The owl always followed instructions and had only recently started to question why.

The meeting that the owl had been told to observe had been called by Jack to discuss the list that Briony had made before her death. Three things remained. One was to give Primrose a specially made scarf, but no one knew for sure where she had gone. They knew Primrose was alive because her name had not erased itself from the list. The other items on the list concerned Evelyn, Briony's youngest sister. She needed to be found and given a scarf too. The trouble with this was that no one had heard of Evelyn since the night of a Great Flood twenty-four years ago. Evelyn was considered lost or dead, but as her name had not disappeared off the list, she too had to be alive.

As a result, after the meeting, the animals had separated into groups to begin a search of the Ancient Forest. Their intention was to listen to old stories and rumours, in the hope the list could be completed and Briony would then miraculously live again.

Now unhappily, the owl realised that the Summoner had not noticed its arrival and definitely wouldn't appreciate being caught off guard. So, as quietly as possible, the bird slipped back out of the entrance hole, found an advantageous perch and tried to discover what was engrossing the Summoner so completely. Dipping its head from side to side it tried to peer in through the hole it had just exited and noticed two boxes. On one box a red light buzzed angrily. On the other box was a screen. The owl recognised a lot of writing but could not work out anything more. To the small bird it made no sense at all.

The Summoner, formless in the dark cloak it always wore, was totally preoccupied with some sort of light source. The light illuminated the Summoner's gaunt face eerily. It had been many years since the owl had seen the Summoner clearly and a cold shiver ran up the bird's back. It had never seen the Summoner so absorbed or animated for such a long time. It felt a bit jealous and unsure what to do next. Normally the owl had the Summoner's complete attention. The bird did not want to think of the repercussions of being caught doing the wrong thing. It had taken the bird a long time to gather up the courage to come back and make the report.

The owl remembered a time, many years ago, when the light source had mysteriously turned darkly quiet. A foul mood had descended on the Summoner for months. The nervous owl hoped this would not happen again.

Becoming bored, the owl once more rehearsed the report in its mind. It had to remember not to mention Briony's bracelet or the magical scarves she had made, as this information had been withheld previously, when it had reported on Briony's funeral. But it still worried - what if the rat was a spy and had already made a report? A rat had taken a rather unusual interest in the owl at the beginning of the meeting at the fallen oak tree and had disappeared without anyone noticing. The owl had to be very careful in what it reported or it was going to be in a lot of pain. So the bird paced up and down on a branch outside the hole, miserable and unsure what to do next.

Coming to a decision, the owl took off effortlessly and glided gracefully above the tall tree. It then hooted loudly, before swooping down and entering the hole to land on its perch.

Fluffing out its feathers, the owl tried to relax and waited for the Summoner's instructions. It noted the way one long, bony finger turned off the red light that buzzed so annoyingly, killing the sound instantly. It then watched curiously as the other box-like thing was quickly covered up. It was so obvious that the Summoner wanted to keep them hidden. Trying to act as calmly as possible, the owl started to preen its soft feathers and waited for the Summoner to ask for its report.

'I don't believe I summoned you,' the Summoner said coldly.

'The meeting, you...' the owl muttered miserably; horribly aware that things were beginning to go desperately wrong.

'Ah yes, I forgot...' the Summoner added, looking back in the direction of the covered boxes.

The owl was stunned; the Summoner had never, ever forgotten anything. Something important must have happened today.

'Don't dawdle, speak up! Be quick about it!' the Summoner ordered, irritated and annoyed at the owl's interruption.

'The hunt for Primrose and Evelyn is on, all parts of the river are to be searched, lots of animals helping. Rabbits are getting nervous. Orion may have found his pack. Jack and friends are meeting at Briony's resting place on the evening of the next Full Moon. Story of the flood discussed. Fear that someone called Darius might have survived,' the owl stopped for breath.

'And?'

The owl felt the cold stare of the Summoner's eyes even though it couldn't see them and began to shiver.

The Summoner went to press the button that would have sent a painful charge through the silver chain, but found the chain dangled loosely. Sighing with frustration and annoyance at finding the owl was not secured properly to its perch, the Summoner placed long, bony fingers around the bird's neck and squeezed gently.

'And?' the cruel voice repeated.

'I've done something stupid,' the owl confessed nervously.

The evil laugh that the Summoner emitted ran ice cold through the owl's veins.

'Tell me!'

'I got spotted. They chose me. I was careless,' the owl stuttered, becoming increasingly scared as the fingers tightened around its throat.

'And what did my sweet, little bird promise to do?' the Summoner asked, releasing the pressure around the owl's neck. The change in the Summoner's tone was sickly sweet; scarier than the usual cold, clipped tones.

'They want me to send and take messages between the groups

as they search for Evelyn and Primrose,' the owl choked, as the fingers around its throat tightened again.

The Summoner's laugh was loud and long.

Finally, after a long, uncomfortable silence in which the owl imagined all sorts of horrors, the Summoner spoke in a tone of such deathly quietness and with such menace that it caused the poor owl to tremble violently in fear.

'I told you not to interfere.'

The owl felt cold.

'I told you not to be seen.'

The owl felt sick.

'You know what happens to things that don't do as I say...'

The Summoner released his grasp on the owl's neck and reached for the chain. The owl began to shiver. The Summoner laughed evilly, greatly amused at the poor bird's discomfort.

'I'm just playing with you sweetie, you did well.'

The owl was having trouble gaining control; it was dizzy and nauseous and couldn't work out if the Summoner was being serious or not. The unpredictability of the Summoner's moods was playing havoc on its nerves.

'These messages come to me first, understand?' the Summoner demanded, tightening his grasp on the owl's neck again and using the familiar, unemotional tone.

The owl nodded, understanding only too well.

'Now, go!'

Greatly relieved, the bird prepared to fly off and had just become airborne, when the Summoner grabbed at one of its wings. It fluttered desperately, trying hard to regain its balance.

'Never, ever come back here unless summoned. If the message

is important, fly to the topmost branch and hoot loudly three times. Understand?'

The owl tried to nod, but the physical exhaustion of trying to fly with just one wing was taking an enormous strain on its overstretched muscles. The Summoner carelessly and thoughtlessly flung the bird from the opening and turned back towards the boxes.

The owl sat trembling on the topmost branch of the tree. As far as it was concerned, the Summoner had hurt it for the last time. Taking time to rest and get its thoughts together, the owl tried to sleep. It needed daylight for the task it had been assigned to do.

As the morning sun cast its warming rays on the top of the forest trees, the owl awoke. Flexing its wings, the owl noticed something sparkle at its feet. It looked down. The silver clasp that circled its foot had just caught the light from the rising sun. The small bird sighed deeply. It resented the clasp that bound it to its jailor and wanted rid of it, but then it saw something wonderful - the clasp was loose! It must have happened while it had been hung upside down. Seizing the silver clasp in its sharp beak, it severed it with one bite and flung it as far away as possible.

Freedom! The owl was free. It could never, ever be summoned again!

Taking to the air, still very unsettled, it flew off to find a friendly face - Velvet the mole. It did not look back.

Meanwhile, at the base of the tallest tree in the forest, a brown rat with dark, beady eyes took that shiny, silver clasp between its long, sharp, front teeth and scuttled off into the undergrowth, believing its mistress might find it to be very important.

3. INSIDE THE ANCIENT TREE

Waiting in total darkness, Primrose tried her hardest to remain calm. As she sat, she hugged her knees to her chest. She felt as though she was being tested, something was waiting for her to lose her temper and start to scream and shout. She sat quietly and listened, remembering the voice and the words that had been whispered to her as she had left the cottage garden - she was certain it had been Briony, her aunt, telling her not to give up. Primrose had no intention of giving up, but that did not stop the growing unease she felt at the continued silence and darkness that surrounded her.

At first, Primrose thought she was hearing things, a low buzzing noise like an alarm going off sounded, but it stopped as she became conscious of it. Next, she heard soft creaking noises. It reminded her of the noises in Briony's cottage when she had slept over on the rare occasions - 'settling', Briony had called it, explaining that the house was relaxing after a long day. The idea of a house needing to rest after a long day had amused Primrose. Houses did not live; they were just a place to eat, sleep and grow.

Primrose was momentarily startled, above her head pin pricks of light started to appear. She blinked hard, hoping that the darkness was about to fade, but that did not stop her heart from beating faster from a sudden attack of nervous anticipation. The lights flickered. Primrose slowed her breathing and told herself to relax. The lights reminded her of the sparklers she had held on bonfire nights. However these lights did not dim but gradually became brighter, and slowly the inside of the Ancient Tree was revealed.

Primrose looked around cautiously, giving her eyes time to adjust to the light. As she took everything in, she marvelled at what she saw.

The inside walls of the Tree had been planed and polished to an incredible smoothness. Ornately decorated murals were carved into the walls, depicting multiple forest scenes. Each one coloured in the rich, natural colours of ancient wood - deep oranges, a plethora of browns, warm reds and yellows.

The soft lighting complimented the décor; homely, comforting and welcoming. Looking up at the ceiling, Primrose noticed winding ivy had been etched into beams that met in the centre, from which a beautiful chandelier hung. Tiny, crystal roses dangled delicately from it and glittered brightly with many lights, like luminous fire flies. A stairway spiralled majestically in front of her, hugging the contours of the Tree. The bannister and newels were carved similarly to the wooden beams and the top of the bottommost post had been skilfully decorated with a single, perfect rose. Primrose was speechless.

A kitchen area was situated on Primrose's left, from which a truly, appetising aroma wafted and tickled her nose; it made her stomach grumble loudly in both anticipation and appreciation. Along with the Aga and work area, a heavy, wooden table stood with two bench seats, waxed to highlight the natural wood grain to perfection.

On Primrose's right there was a comfortable sitting room, with elegantly carved chairs adorned with deep, red, velvet cushions. They seemed to beckon her weary body to take a seat and relax, but Primrose would not sully their plushness with her unwashed body.

Primrose slowly stood up. Her muscles were stiff from staying still for so long, but she ignored the pain. She was totally in awe at everything she saw and decided to explore upstairs.

Her fingers lovingly caressed the exquisitely carved rose on the first post. As she touched the rose, soft lights lit each riser; highlighting each tread. She carefully placed each foot on each stair, thankful for the red, thick-piled carpet. She had no wish to scratch or dirty anything in this truly remarkable place. She couldn't help it, she trailed her fingers gently along the inside wall and lovingly stoked the artistically carved bannister. She wished she had washed her hands first, but as her hand or finger made a mark, it magically disappeared!

At the top of the stairs, there was a door. On that door a name was carved - Primrose. Tears started to trickle slowly down her face. Her throat tightened as emotions she had not experienced in ages washed over her. She opened *her* door with the gentlest of touches to reveal a magnificent carved canopied bed with soft, cream furnishings and a bathroom through a partly opened door. Primrose knew she was home.

She noticed another staircase that led to another floor upstairs, but Primrose was only interested in the bathroom. She needed a wash desperately; the odour of fish and river water no longer suited the place she found herself in. Primrose wanted a bath. She wanted to wash away the dirt and grime embedded in her skin.

Entering the bathroom, Primrose noticed a white scalloped bath with a matching suite. She thought how wonderful it would be to soak in a deep, perfumed, soapy bath. To her amazement the faucets turned on, and warm water started to gush and gurgle into the deep bath. The scent of lavender filled the air. It was her favourite perfume. Amazing!

Primrose jumped violently. A grey figure was staring at her intently from the other side of the room and looked as shocked as she was. Primrose stepped forward, so did the grey figure. Primrose clenched her fists and was about to speak. The grey figure did the same. Primrose felt stupid as she realised that she was looking at her reflection in a long mirror, and laughed shakily, embarrassed by her mistake.

A truly horrific, filthy face stared back at her; spiky tufts of matted, dirty hair stuck out and framed her grubby face, which was engraved with deep, black lines, while purple-white streaks of dried, encrusted bird's mess zig-zagged their way through her spiky hair and down her face.

She began to laugh loudly and wildly; tears ran down her cheeks adding to the mess that already coated her dry skin. She remembered a time when her mother, Violette, had said she was a mess. Now she knew how wrong her mother had been; her mother had no idea how messy, messy could be and for some unknown and inexplicable reason, Primrose found this extremely funny.

Primrose continued her examination; her clothes were grey, filthy, worn and smelt of fish and sweat. From her waist down, she was slightly cleaner, due to her prolonged contact with the river, and she could see faint traces of pink where her skin should be. But, most amazing of all was the stone monstrosity of a foot. It was definitely smaller and shaped more like an actual foot and no longer resembled a concrete block. Primrose had no idea how that had happened.

Primrose looked at the bath and thought it was going to take more than one immersion to get rid of the years of thick dirt that encrusted her body and change her back into some kind of recognisable being. It was time though to make that transition.

As she soaked in the warm, soapy, perfumed bathwater, she noticed above her head, an intricate carving of three young women with children. She briefly wondered who they were, but tonight she was going to relax, get clean, eat some of that hearty, wonderfully smelling broth that continued to send appetising wafts up the stairs, and then sleep in that comfortable, soft looking bed. A detailed exploration of her new home could wait until tomorrow.

Primrose did not know why or how she knew it, but she was absolutely certain that this wonderful, amazing place was hers and hers alone. The Ancient Tree had let her in and welcomed her home. All Primrose had had to do was find the way in and show a bit of patience; the Tree was doing the rest. She did not know to whom she spoke, but she said it anyway - thank you.

4. PRIMROSE HAS A SURPRISE
OR TWO

Two adults looked down on a peaceful family scene set in the forest, next to a stream. Two young women sat on the rocks. Each woman bounced a young child on their lap as one man looked on fondly. In the background, another younger woman seemed to be tickling trout in a small stream with another man; he appeared to be laughing at her attempts to catch one. Something else seemed to be staring down at the family group, but Primrose was unable to make out what it was exactly, due to the fragrant clouds of steam wafting above her head. Whatever it was, it gave her an unpleasant feeling.

Primrose lay soaking in yet another bath, determined to rid her skin of all the filth that still stained parts of her face and arms. The scent of lavender filled the air. Primrose breathed in deeply and sunk below the frothy bubbles, before studying the carving once more.

She thought that the two older adults must be dead as they looked down from the clouds, but she was sure she recognised one of the men as Jack or at least a younger version of him. That meant that the woman next to him was probably a younger

Briony, which also meant that they had had a child, which could not be Elina, since the time line would be wrong... unless the other couple had had twins.

She wondered if the other woman was Violette or Vile Vi, her mother, as Primrose liked to call her. Primrose sneered at the thought and her stone foot, which hung over the bath, throbbed painfully. The foot had a tendency to ache when she thought less charitably towards things.

If the woman was Violette, could Primrose be the child that seemed to enjoy being bounced on its mother's knee? Could the man that laughed at the girl tickling trout be her father, she wondered. Her stone foot tingled and ached pleasantly as she thought of the endless possibilities. They were obviously relatives of some sort. Primrose looked at the foot and sighed, it seemed to be talking to her now; perhaps she should add that to its ever-growing list of uses.

Once more, she sunk under the scented bubbles and immersed her body in the warm water, certain that she was one of the babies depicted in the carving. Her head spun with that idea, someone had definitely tampered with time. How could her mother have looked so young and Briony so worn and aged? How could she still be so young? Had her mother used magic to keep them both young? If so, why hadn't Briony used her magic to do the same for herself?

As she dried herself, she lifted her eyes to the carving once more and wondered who the other girl was that played in the river. She thought that maybe that was her, but Primrose looked down at her foot and felt nothing. She looked at the bouncing child and once more her foot tingled.

Primrose promised herself she would look at all the other

wooden carvings the Ancient Tree possessed and search for more clues as to whom these people were. But as her stomach growled noisily, she knew breakfast beckoned.

What should she treat herself to this morning, she wondered? Once Briony had made her a lovely, creamy porridge drizzled with fresh honey, it had been absolutely delicious. How lovely it would be to savour and enjoy that special moment again?

Back in her room, Primrose had another surprise - a cupboard full of clothes. How the Tree knew her size baffled her, but Primrose was not going to complain. She gratefully chose a brand-new outfit - black jeggings and a yellow blouse. There was no way she wanted to wear the clothes of the day before, she had been wearing that particular outfit for thirteen years!

However, that was not the only surprise waiting for Primrose, when she entered the kitchen, she discovered another of her wishes had come true - breakfast! Primrose so loved this magical Tree.

As she savoured every morsel of the wonderful, honeyed porridge, she once again took in her surroundings. There were lots of carvings that needed to be studied, but there were two things that continued to draw her attention.

The first was a beautifully carved rocking cradle, and the second was a panel situated near the entrance; it was marked with an inexplicable design, almost like a burn. Both aroused her curiosity, but first she needed a drink and this time she was determined to make it herself. She was not prepared to let the Ancient Tree indulge her, at least not all of the time! She smiled as a thought flitted through her mind - the idea that she could become so lazy and never move again for yet another decade or so, but this time it would be due to piling on the pounds and not from being turned stone!

Standing at the foot of the cradle, tears gently started to trace their way down her cheeks. Ornately engraved in ancient lettering was the name 'Primrose'. She was at a loss, emotion welled up as she realised this was indeed the cradle in which she would have slept as a baby. What dreadful thing had happened to her for her past to be taken away from her so cruelly? She must have been truly loved for this to have been carved just for her.

Tentatively, she stretched her right hand out to caress her name. As her fingers lovingly stroked the letters, the feeling of a million butterflies fluttering their wings danced daintily at her finger tips. Flecks of golden dust materialised in front of her eyes. Primrose stepped back in shock, brought her hand close to her face and watched the sparkling dust float away, totally mesmerised.

'That's so cool,' she gasped and delicately traced an arc through the air and watched spellbound as a golden rainbow formed.

'I have magic,' she marvelled.

Once more, she looked at the cradle and leant towards it. After placing her left hand on the top rail she felt short, sharp pains travel up her arm. She then felt a violent onslaught of pins and needles that stung viciously like wasps travel up her arm. From the finger tips of her left hand trailed a thin wisp of grey smoke. She grabbed the aching limb with her right hand and the pain disappeared as quickly as it came.

Primrose was terrified. She looked at both hands, both hands looked normal, both hands held magic. How on earth was she supposed to handle this? She had no one to guide her. This was definitely not so cool. She looked around blindly and implored, 'Tell me! What am I supposed to do now?'

On the other side of the room, a rocking chair started to move and creak. Primrose took the cue and went to sit down. She needed to calm down, think logically, contemplate this last revelation and let the Tree guide her. She closed her eyes and rocked gently to and fro until her nerves calmed.

Opening her eyes, Primrose looked back at the cradle. The workmanship was remarkable, the carvings intricate and beautiful. Hundreds of primroses decorated the spindles and rails, but one panel on its side depicted one whole flower. The outline of the panel glinted slightly, as though it had caught the sunlight, but there was no sunlight inside the Ancient Tree!

Once more, Primrose approached the cradle to study the flower more closely. There seemed to be a small protrusion, barely visible in the middle of the flower; she pressed it with a finger on her right hand - she dared not use her left! A small click was heard and the whole panel moved slightly to reveal a secret drawer.

Carefully, gently, still using only her right hand, which seemed to be behaving itself and emitting no magic, she pulled the drawer open and saw three things: a letter addressed to her, a silver bracelet with a solitary diamond shaped like a primrose and an ancient embossed book with magical symbols titled 'Harnessing Magic'.

'You wonderful, wonderful Tree,' Primrose spoke aloud, as relief flooded through her body and the fear that had started to engulf her began to subside.

She picked up the three items, reverently, and took them

to the table and sat down on one of the bench seats. She held up the bracelet, appreciated its beauty and knew for certain it belonged to her. She slipped it onto her left wrist; it seemed the right thing to do, and then she carefully opened the letter and began to read.

Dearest Primrose, our ray of sunshine,

Know that I and your father loved you dearly. You were the most perfect of babies, always ready with a smile or a chuckle whenever we held you. It breaks my heart to know that if you are reading this, I am not in this world and nor is your father, that we failed to protect you.

Tonight, your father and I have just received a message, a plea for help. My magic and your father's expert knowledge are required to prevent an impending flood. Beavers further upstream are behaving bizarrely and endangering life.

The weather lately has been atrocious, there will be floods and the beavers are holding too much water in the Forest Lake and making matters dangerous. Our home is threatened.

I have not got much time for explanations, so please forgive my haste and take heed of what I write. It is important.

For your protection, place the bracelet on the wrist you feel or know it needs to go on. There is a huge likelihood you will inherit both types of magic. Read the Ancient Tome, from the beginning to the end. It is imperative you don't skip, miss or ignore any page. Something lurks in this world, which has threatened our family once before, and although it was beaten back, it was not vanquished. I feel it is building again.

If you feel that strange, inexplicable things have been

happening recently, don't venture outside until you have mastered the Invisibility and Barrier Protection Spells. You will find a yellow cloak that will give the temporary protection of invisibility. It can be found on the third floor. Keep yourself hidden at all times.

The Tree and Tome will reveal extra secrets as you read and master your magic.

It pains me that this letter is filled with dire warnings, but I have an uneasy feeling about tonight - something feels wrong - a premonition perhaps.

Be on your guard, let others earn your trust and trust your feelings - your inner self. Again, I can't stress the importance of keeping your presence and identity a secret from strangers. Stay hidden. Use the cloak and the magic.

I promise you, we will meet again and probably in the most unexpected of places.

Know that we love you, with all our hearts and souls, to the furthest stars and back.

Till we meet again

XXXX

P.S. If possible I will endeavour to give you a sign as you finish reading this letter. Keep the letter and Tome hidden in the drawer. It will open only for you and me.

Primrose looked up, once more tears streamed down her face. She let out a heart-breaking sob but saw and sensed nothing. Bitterly disappointed, she was about to screw the letter into the tightest of balls, when she smelled something - the sweet smell of roses filled the air around her and then she felt the warmest of hugs. Her senses heightened - the scent was oddly familiar. She sensed the comfort it offered and succumbed to it. Her body relaxed, and she seemed to float and fade.

Primrose panicked. She felt something pulling at her. She fought against the feeling and opened her eyes. Her relief was enormous, everything felt normal again and the scent of roses had faded. Something confused her though; the smell of roses was not one of the perfumes her mother had used, so, why did it seem so familiar to her? And more worryingly, why had she felt as though something was trying to take her away from the Ancient Tree?

Primrose stood up and placed her mother's letter next to the Ancient Tome, her hands itched to flick through the pages, but she knew the word imperative had been written differently for a reason. She needed to calm her nerves.

It was time to examine the third floor.

From her bedroom, she slowly climbed the smaller staircase, which was still decorated as richly as the first one. The stairs spiralled more tightly, keeping to the curvature of the Tree. She reached a door and rubbed her hands down the sides of her black jeggings, for some unexplained reason they felt clammy.

Slowly, she opened the door to reveal a small circular room - a cloakroom that tapered upwards to a trap door. Primrose thought she must have reached the top of the Ancient Tree by now. Around the walls various coats hung from carved wooden pegs, depicting the heads of different forest creatures. On one peg, a beautiful leather belt hung with a silver clasp shaped like a wolf's head, with two brilliant diamonds for its eyes. Various types of footwear were arranged orderly and in pairs under the coats. In front of her was a full-length mirror, with a yellow cloak hung next to it.

Staring back at her was her cleaner self. Short, golden hair outlined her face, and the spiky look and grime had gone. Her skin was extremely pale due to the lack of attention from the sun, and her cheeks were puffy from recent shed tears.

Primrose almost did not recognise herself. She noticed with surprise that she was quite pretty and that she seemed to look older than the figure that had stared back at her the night before. Maybe, she had not been mad but correct when she had considered the idea that Vile Vi had actually been tampering with time. Now, that she was out of her mother's jurisdiction and no longer a statue - time might be catching up with her. This thought unsettled her a bit; just how old would she be the next time she looked at herself?

The yellow cloak hung from a peg next to the mirror; according to her mother's letter, this should be the Cloak of Invisibility. She stretched out her hand and removed it; surprised by how light and delicate it felt.

She swung it round her shoulders and her reflection from the neck down disappeared. Just her head, disembodied, floated in the air. Primrose giggled for the first time that day and jiggled about; amused to see her head float around the room. She could not help it, but the desire to play about was over-whelming. To her head she added the odd hand, leg or foot, making them appear and disappear at random. She had never seen anything so funny. Finally, she slipped the hood over her head and disappeared completely.

Hidden behind the cloak, a wooden ladder was fixed against

the wall and led upwards to the trap door. Primrose decided the only way to go was up.

Standing on the roof of the world, Primrose took in the 360-degree view. The entire forest could be seen from this excellent vantage point and to her delight no one could see her or would even realise she was there. She stood quietly, breathed in the clean, fresh air and listened to the wind dance around the boughs, branches, twigs and newly unfurling leaves. She had never felt so alive.

A sudden, faint noise reached her ears and she turned towards the sound - just the wind she thought, trying to free itself from the interlacing branches. Primrose saw a small hole in one of the topmost branches emit a small puff of dirt, she smiled, as she realised she must be sharing her home with a woodpecker and had just missed it. As she looked around, her eyes spotted a small, reddish-brown owl. The owl threw something onto the ground and flew off. It did not look back.

As she turned to go back inside, her eye caught sight of a metal contraption hidden amongst some vines. She noticed it was some sort of pulley. Could this be another way down to the forest floor, she wondered. But that discovery would have to wait; it was time to go back in, she had some reading to do and a panel to investigate.

Back in the main room of the Ancient Tree, Primrose stood and stared at the strange markings on the panel, near the trap hatch. She had a strange feeling that the Ancient Tree was trying to tell her something, but she had no idea what it was. To her, the marks resembled angry, reddened scars radiating outwards from a central point. The centre was slightly concave and blackened, as though something must have hit it with tremendous force. She couldn't help wondering how the markings were made.

A blast of energy suddenly surged past her, catching her unawares. It twisted her slightly and then smashed against the panel. It ricocheted around the room and burst through the trap door and out of the Tree.

Both of Primrose's hands lifted against her will and stretched towards the panel, the left hand more dominant in its need to touch it. The bracelet throbbed. Primrose maintained control - just - she forced her right hand to take hold of the bracelet and brought both hands down to her waist.

Breathing deeply, she tried to calm her shredded nerves and turned her back on the panel. She told herself that this strange event was the result of some kind of residual energy. The Ancient Tree had tried to tell her what might have happened in the past, but she was still none the wiser. She really must remember, in future, to be more careful of what she wished for. The Ancient Tree had an uncanny way of reading her thoughts and bringing them to life in extreme and very unpredictable ways.

On the floor, near the trap door, she noticed a moth fluttering around in circles; it seemed disorientated and must have felt the sudden surge of energy too. She bent down and gently guided it into her right hand and then placed it carefully onto the kitchen table, away from the energy trail. The moth paused, appeared to look at her and then flew away. She never saw it again.

She felt her stone foot throb; she had been on her feet too long.

Primrose looked at the panel once more, she was not going to touch or go near it again, at least not until she knew how to control her magic, without putting herself in danger.

Absent-mindedly, she rubbed her left hand and a memory returned; she had seen Briony do the same thing once on one of her 'Awakenings'. The 'Awakenings' were times when Briony would change her back to human form, and see if she was ready to apologise and change her ways, but Primrose had taken great delight in unnerving Briony instead. Primrose had sensed a weakness and couldn't help but take her anger and frustration out on her. Now, she felt vaguely uneasy about those times. Primrose had not been kind to Briony. She wondered whether Briony had had both kinds of magic as well and had been scared of it and her? Silently, Primrose mouthed the word 'sorry'.

Primrose sighed, there was nothing she could do about the past, but she could make up for it in the future. She had some serious reading to do: she needed to fully understand her magic and for the first time ever she was going to follow her mother's instructions - she would read that Tome starting at page one and not skip a page. She was convinced her life depended on it. She picked up the Tome and walked towards the plush, comfortable, red seats to begin her study: the importance of controlling her magic was paramount.

It was not until she sat down, that she realised she had actually walked with two feet! She had actually walked properly with two, perfectly formed, wonderful feet. As she stared at them, delighted in the rejuvenation of her right foot, she wriggled her toes and once more found herself crying, but this time the tears were of joy, relief and happiness.

It suddenly dawned on her that the transformation of her right foot had been a gradual affair. She had felt the first tingle when she had allowed the baby otter to snuggle against her for warmth. She also thought she had felt something when her thoughts had praised Victor for his persistence in his search for her. Even when she had never given up trying to find the entrance into the Tree, she had noticed a difference in her foot; especially as she had not lost her temper - a rare thing for her when she became angry.

That morning she had also helped a disorientated moth, and agreed to take her mother's advice. More importantly, she had also said sorry for the way she had treated Briony. Primrose briefly wondered what would happen if she reverted back to her old ways and felt the dull ache and a heaviness invade her foot again. She smiled; Briony had been extremely clever when she had cast that spell.

Stretching out her long, slender legs, Primrose settled more comfortably onto the sofa and started to read. Occasionally - no, let's be truthful here - often giving her right foot a sneaky glance, just to make sure. She had never been happier.

5. VICTOR EXAMINES THE OTTERS' HOLE

The small owl hovered above the heads of Velvet and Victor and wondered what they were up to. They were behaving extremely oddly next to a partially hidden hole in the steep river bank. Victor was dangling rather precariously from a thin branch; swinging erratically, his legs seemed to be trying to grab or feel for a purchase on the near vertical bank. The owl thought the fragile branch would break at any moment and result in Victor falling unceremoniously into the river. Velvet was shouting out various words of instructions, which seemed to be aggravating Victor to no end.

'Left a bit, right a bit, nearly there, pity. You just missed it that time. No, left a bit - not that much! You nearly had it that time!'

Landing lightly and quietly on the bank next to Velvet, the owl peered inquisitively over the edge.

'That's it!' Velvet squeaked excitedly, peering short-sightedly down the bank.

Victor missed his target once more.

'Shame, you were so close,' Velvet commiserated.

'He's going to get dizzy swinging about like that or pull his arms out of his sockets. What's he trying to do?' the owl asked, moving its head side to side, matching Victor's swings.

'Hey, Owl! Good to see you. Did you know he's scared of water? Didn't tell me that until he went over the edge.' Velvet giggled in amusement, feeling that it was about time someone else got wet other than himself. Velvet had been soaked twice recently, once by an overturned bird bath and another time by a jug of orange at one of Elina's picnics.

'Some guidance down here would be appreciated,' Victor called, his voice rising in mounting panic. The water looked extremely deep to him and very cold. He was beginning to think that that was where he was heading, and very shortly by the look of things.

'Couldn't give him a nudge in the right direction, could you?' Velvet queried, 'Your eyesight has got to be better than mine.'

'Depends if he's going right or left,' the owl remarked gravely, still moving its head from side to side in time with Victor's swings.

'Into the hole would be much appreciated,' Velvet laughed, 'it's the otters' home or it might have been until Primrose scared them away. It's the only place Victor didn't search. He wants to make sure she didn't hide in there.'

'Velvet, if you don't do something soon I'm going to fall!' Victor's voice screeched from below.

'Don't panic. Help is on the way,' Velvet replied.

The owl flexed its wings; then rose gracefully and effortlessly into the air. Silently and swiftly it swooped downwards and aimed at the alarmed Victor.

Victor was startled. Out of the corner of his eye he saw a

bird hurtling towards him. Knowing nothing of Velvet's plan, he knew he was too big to be carried away, but he could always be knocked from this thin, fragile branch to which he hung onto so tenaciously. Victor didn't fancy being torn into smaller chunks as he lay injured on the bank below. If he'd been able to climb, he would have been up that branch like a shot; instead he closed his eyes, hoped for the best and prayed for a quick and painless end.

The owl's timing was perfect; its talons collided with Victor's back just as the swing took him past the hole. Then swerving expertly, the owl once more returned to Velvet's side, swivelled its head, so its ears could pick up the slightest of sounds below.

On landing, Victor knew he'd had a miraculous escape. Poking his head out of the hole, he watched the owl move towards Velvet and recognised with relief their appointed messenger. He felt a wave of gratitude at its timely arrival and a wave of irritation towards Velvet at his lack of expertise in the art of communication.

Victor shook himself out, stretched out his aching muscles, and not for the first time wished he had sent Velvet over the edge. At least, if Velvet had fallen, he was accustomed to the occasional soaking. However, he knew that Velvet would have taken an age to search the hole and spent even more time in getting there and back. Velvet's slow pace and laid-back attitude irritated him at times.

On entering the hole, Victor's stomach convulsed violently, the smell of decaying fish and damp was overpowering. Determined not to give up on this quest, Victor continued his search - the hole needed to be examined thoroughly.

As Victor meticulously searched inside the dark, dank lair,

the owl enquired if there were any special messages that needed to be delivered. Velvet shrugged his shoulders, 'Best to wait for Victor, he's the one to ask, but so far we've found out nothing new and we've asked all sorts of animals. All their stories just mention the five Ds: death, debris, dirt and dark dust. It's all getting a bit tiring actually.'

From below a vibration was felt travelling through the ground; Victor's powerful legs drummed out a signal letting Velvet know his search had been completed. Velvet once more peered over the edge and could just make out the blurry form of Victor. He seemed to be very agitated, which Velvet thought was strange as nothing seemed to have flustered him before.

'What's up, Victor?'

'Get me up!' Victor shouted, 'Primrose was here!'

'How, I can't lift you?' Velvet replied, flabbergasted. Victor surely didn't think he was capable of lifting him.

'Well, I can't very well stay here. She might come back.'

'You could always fly,' the owl suggested helpfully.

'You trying to be funny,' Victor snapped, being uncharacteristically rude.

Although Victor believed Primrose had only used this place once, he was still feeling extremely vulnerable. He looked at the mud slide and thought back to the day when he had considered it would be fun to slide down it. Now, as he looked down, he felt differently. The otters' slipway was steeper than he had first thought and the river looked cold, deep and uninviting. He looked around, maybe there was another way up to Velvet, but he couldn't see one.

Too many rocks, bushes and branches blocked Victor's view. He was fast coming to the conclusion that he had no alternative, but to jump and take a swim for the first time in his life. He found this idea more than a little bit daunting. Hares were not born to swim!

The owl, on hearing no further instructions or pleas for help, took off to observe. After all, that had been its job once. It noticed Victor looking around frantically and giving quick nervous glances towards the river. Gliding smoothly alongside the river bank, the owl spied a possible route that Victor might be able to use.

'Follow my flight path with your eyes,' the owl called out to him, 'there's a ledge to your left. Can you see it?'

'Not sure, can you hover just above it?' Victor asked.

Victor watched the owl carefully and noticed the ledge was a boulder and a good jump away.

'Bit of a jump,' Victor answered, 'might be able to do it.'

'If you can't, I can always give you another push!' the owl responded with a small hoot of laughter.

'At least you've given me a warning this time,' Victor laughed back, his nerves calming down a bit, knowing he had an escape route that didn't involve getting wet, 'show me again where I have to land.'

Victor leaned backwards and prepared to launch himself forwards by using his hind legs as powerful springs. He watched the owl as it hovered above his soon-to-be landing spot, tensed and sprang suddenly with all his might.

As Victor flew towards his target, the owl soared quickly to get out of his way. Victor landed perfectly on his front legs, his hind legs following rapidly behind him; the impetus sent him head over heels into a gorse bush. He emerged slowly, a little embarrassed, shook out his ears, brushed himself down and glared in the direction of Velvet, who was laughing hysterically above him.

'Told you, you could fly,' the owl hooted wisely, as Victor followed a now visible trail up to the top of the river bank.

Once they were altogether, Velvet asked Victor what he had found in the otters' hole and why he was so positive that Primrose had indeed hidden there.

'Along with lots of smelly, rotten, decaying fish, I found this…' Victor spat out a dirty, grey piece of material; which showed a glimpse of bright yellow.

'This was hers!' he announced importantly. 'Everything at the back of that small hole was flattened, by that stone foot of hers. That's where I found that piece of material. I also discovered a groove scratched into the floor, leading from the back of the cave to the opening. I reckon that was made by that foot of hers as well, always leaving an easy trail to follow. She definitely hid there, but where she is now, I've no idea.'

Victor turned towards the owl, their messenger, 'Owl, can you find Jack and tell him our news? Trouble is, I don't know where he is either. He's looking for Primrose's scarf, thinks he's dropped it in the forest somewhere.'

The owl couldn't believe its ears, that wonderful, amazing scarf, gone! How it would have loved to have possessed something as beautiful as that? The owl nearly took off immediately to search for it and keep it, if only it could be found. The owl would never have been so careless.

Velvet interrupted the bird's thoughts. He had to ask the owl twice, as it had been so completely preoccupied with the thought of Primrose's lost scarf.

'What's your name?' Velvet repeated.

'I'm an owl,' the bird answered simply.

'You must have a name. Are you a boy or a girl?'

The owl shrugged its shoulders and simply repeated, 'I'm an owl.'

'Who do you fly and play with?' Velvet continued; he was full of curiosity about their new companion.

'No one, I have no friends,' the owl said miserably, then looked at both of them and asked eagerly and excitedly, 'Will you be my friends?'

'You're working with us, so of course we're your friends. And friends have to have names,' Velvet exclaimed happily, 'what name would you like?'

'I like the name Eve,' the owl replied shyly, 'it will remind me of when I saw you first, in the eve…ning.'

Velvet giggled at the owl's joke.

'You must be a girl then, as Eve's a girl's name. So Eve it is!' Velvet stated happily.

'Don't be ridiculous, Velvet,' Victor remarked impatiently, with sarcasm, stamping his foot in annoyance. 'Owl can't be Eve. We're looking for an Eve. I can just see us asking the next animal we meet, "Have you seen someone called Eve, we have lost her," and they will say, "She's standing there, next to you." We will be the laughing stock of the forest and cause so much confusion. So she can't be Eve or Lyn or…' Victor stared sternly at both of them, '…or Evelyn either, understood?'

The owl looked disappointed, Velvet looked a trifle embarrassed; he thought he had been a little bit silly, and now he had also disappointed their new friend as well.

'But we've got to call her something,' he mumbled, 'how

about Dawn? That name can remind you when we took our first flight together and the start of our friendship,' suggested Velvet, now feeling much better.

Smiling happily and strutting proudly, Owl finally had a name and friends. Friends she had once spied on and been forced to tell the Summoner everything about. Perhaps that was something she should keep to herself. She did not want to lose her new friends as soon as she had found them.

The owl, or Dawn as she was now called, felt happiness for the first time in her life. She was not going to be lonely ever again, but this happiness she felt was spoiled by another feeling - guilt. She knew friends should be honest with each other, but she dared not. Sometimes, perhaps, it was best to keep somethings secret. So Dawn decided it would be best to keep her past to herself!

6. DILLY HAS A PROBLEM

Dilly was extremely unhappy, because she did not fit in; the other wolves did not like her. Her father, Orion, had finally been reunited with his parents, Antares and Elektra and his lost pack. As Orion and Ebony struck up new friendships and spent time getting to know his aging parents, Dilly felt pushed out. Dilly found herself without proper friends, amongst strangers that did not trust her and in a different forest, located just outside the Ancient Forest in which she had been born. It looked different, it smelled different and she was different; marked by a dreadful scar, caused by Primrose's stone foot. She felt alienated and lonely.

Even Junior had moved on and spent time establishing himself within the hierarchy of the pack, which often involved a lot of rough, boisterous play. Junior was determined to be no pushover; he felt he had to prove to himself, his parents and the pack that he was strong, brave, fearless and dependable. He used his time improving his hunting, fighting and stalking skills, often pitting his strength against the other older, male wolves. Junior was determined Primrose would never get the better of him again.

Although Dilly had tried to mix with the pack, she found

it impossible. Whenever she approached them without her family being present, they turned on her; not with their teeth or claws but with their body language and remarks, as well as their silences and looks. Dilly was made to feel very uncomfortable; the pack did not trust her. They considered her to be tainted, because of that huge, ugly scar that disfigured her side.

Messages had been received from rabbits; they had travelled through the ground warning animals of a she-wolf with a horrifying wound that had healed over-night; it had been caused by a witch called Primrose. Anyone associating with Dilly would be in danger. Any normal wolf would have died outright with such an injury; therefore Dilly could not be normal. Dilly was bad luck. Dilly was shunned. The wolf pack took the rabbits' warnings seriously; they were scared of her; certain she had magic. They did their best to try and scare her away.

When Dilly approached her mother and told her of her fears, Ebony felt that her daughter was exaggerating the pack's behaviour and that she would settle in time. Even so, Ebony had secretly watched the wolves on several occasions and had witnessed no bullying or intimidation. Ebony did not want Dilly to think her worries were being ignored. So, she gave her daughter the following advice: be brave, to stand on her own four paws, never show any signs of weakness and remain calm when confronted by bullies.

Dilly had tried. Dilly had tried very hard. She could hold her own against one or two of them, but it was getting harder. She was losing confidence in herself; the pack was wearing her down.

Now, she often took herself off on long walks, preferring her own company and her own thoughts. She considered the idea of running away. Perhaps, she could find Elina and Shadow, her youngest brother. Elina had always treated her nicely. Elina did not care about the scar. Dilly missed Elina and Briony so much. Dilly could not understand this spitefulness against her or the lack of support from her parents and Junior. She felt so alone, as if adrift.

On one of her long walks that took her back into the Ancient Forest, Dilly had found a fantastic resting place, a hidden spot, amongst thick brambles, but in their midst a small, grassy opening where she could enjoy the warmth of the sun. She enjoyed the peace, felt relaxed and sometimes slept soundly; away from prying eyes and cruel jibes.

One day, as she lay dozing, feeling the power of the sun warm her disfigured side (it was strange, but sometimes it felt so cold), she thought of Primrose and was suddenly struck by a strange thought. Primrose had stayed hidden in a 'spot' for years, surrounded by thorny brambles - ugly, forgotten and unloved and here Dilly lay, in a different spot, ugly and alone, all thanks to her!

Dilly felt a surge of pure anger flood through her; this was all Primrose's fault. If Shadow (or Trouble as he was called back then) had not been caught in the brambles, Primrose would never have been found. If Primrose had not hurt Elina, she would not have retaliated and bitten Primrose's foot and then Primrose wouldn't have kicked her and injured her. Furthermore, she would have had friends, lots of them! Dilly hoped the bite she had given Primrose was causing her just as much pain and grief.

Disturbed from her thoughts, Dilly heard faint growls and

rustlings on the other side of the bramble thicket. Her ears twitched. She turned towards the sound, fully alert and her nose identified the intruders quickly - the pack! They had sought her out. Dilly felt her hackles rise and her temper flare.

She was ready to take her mother's advice and stand on her own four paws, but this was not the place to fight, trapped inside a thorny prison. Fuming that the pack had taken away her place of refuge, her only place of safety, she prepared herself to make a final stand against them. She would take the fight to them. After all, if she had been brave enough to bite Primrose and save Elina from further harm, she should be able to take on a few wolves. She could do this.

'She's in here somewhere,' snuffled one wolf excitedly.

'Hiding,' jeered another.

'Frightened and alone, by the smell of it,' laughed a third.

'There's enough of us to give her a real fright this time,' a fourth added smugly, trying his best to be quiet, but at the same time too excited and confident in their numbers to care.

'Remember, no marks, can't afford to get on Orion's bad side. If that upstart thinks he can waltz straight into the alpha role, he's got another fight on his hands,' another wolf stated forcefully.

Dilly recognised that voice and was slightly shocked. The voice belonged to Ursa, her father's older brother, son of Antares - a huge, powerful wolf. She was momentarily stunned that he was the leader of the group that pursued her and it unnerved her. However, she remembered her mother's advice; Dilly would not show them any signs of weakness. She decided to go ahead with her plan.

'We can run her out of the forest. She's bad luck; you've only got to see how Antares and Elektra have aged since she's arrived. They're not going to last much longer and it's all down to her,' Corvus stated forcibly. Corvus was a mature wolf and one to be wary of, he was also Ursa's best friend.

It was Corvus that Dilly had suspected of turning the pack against her. She felt that his remark was totally unfair. What chance did she have against that type of mentality? She could sense the excitement mounting within the pack surrounding her and estimated their numbers to be around six or seven, she was massively outnumbered.

She waited and bided her time until she located their weakest spot - Sasha, a young female wolf, just a bit bigger than her but not as confident. She would become Dilly's escape route. Listening intently, she waited for their signal to attack; that would be her moment to jump out of her hiding place, aiming for Sasha.

The pack had spaced themselves evenly around her and had become quiet. Dilly recognised the signs; any second now the wolves were going to make their move. She felt them tense and a frisson of energy surged through her. Dilly jumped. The pack jumped. Dilly was momentarily saddened as she aimed for Sasha; Sasha had been nice to her at first, but like them all she had turned under the pressure of the others.

Dilly knocked her completely sideways and noticed Sasha fall awkwardly into the spiky brambles. She knew from Shadow's experience how sore those barbs could be, as they stuck and tore into and through fur. It was Sasha or her: Dilly had had no choice. She did not have time to waste on any compassion for Sasha.

Dilly landed lightly and discovered she had more pressing

problems, not all of the wolves had jumped and she had greatly underestimated their numbers. Six jumped, four had not - she now faced four older, experienced male wolves. What chance did she have against them? Time seemed to stand still. She heard the whimpering of the fallen wolf and the disappointed, angry grumblings of the wolves that had jumped and found her missing.

She sensed they were preparing to jump again. Ursa, Corvus and two other wolves turned as one and faced her; their yellow, determined eyes of hostility glared angrily at her. Greatly disadvantaged to make a stand, Dilly turned quickly and ran. She ran as fast as she could. She ran for her life with four angry wolves snapping at her heels, certain in the knowledge that another five wolves would be following close behind and soon.

The forest was unknown to Dilly and the path she had taken was badly overgrown. Bushes tore at her coat viciously, undergrowth snatched at her feet and legs trying to trip her up, but Dilly sped forward, ducking under low, hanging branches, jumping blindly over others, veering sharply around obstacles, but the wolves still followed. She could not shake them from her trail.

Dilly drew in great lungsful of air, she felt her scar pull and her muscles ache, she knew she was running out of time. Up ahead, she saw a wide opening, a gash in the ground - the river!

Pulling on every last vestige of strength left, Dilly jumped wildly. Her front paws landed safely on the other side, but her back legs just missed their footing. Desperately scrambling and pulling with all her might with her front legs she tried to drag her body onto the bank, but her back legs swung hopelessly.

Mud, stones and grass loosened by her struggles fell into the river. Dilly knew by the splashes it was a long way down.

Camouflaged perfectly against the river bank, a brown rat with black, beady eyes watched curiously as a young wolf jumped across the chasm above her head. She watched as the wolf struggled hopelessly to gain a footing. Eyes darting to and fro, ears twitching, the rat heard the pounding feet of an excited wolf pack hurtling in her direction. The rat, although completely unseen, did not wish to stay around and took flight directly, knocking a broken branch purposely sideways, giving Dilly the foothold she desperately needed.

Dilly refused to give up, she swung her legs to gain purchase and finally her back legs found something solid, something that gave her the footing she desperately needed. She sprang. Success! All four feet on the ground, Dilly was running again.

Behind her, she heard two splashes, two wolves had fallen, but the others still pursued her. Ahead lay a forest glade, an opening. Dilly sped towards it. If, she was to fight, it would be in a place where she could move and it might as well be there. She stopped in the middle and turned to face her foes. Eight wolves entered the glade.

Ursa's coat dripped steadily, he had been one of the wolves that had fallen. Now, Ursa wanted Dilly to pay dearly for his embarrassment, falling in front of the pack had not improved his mood.

The sun shone on Dilly, highlighting her silver, black and grey coat. Dilly was a fine-looking wolf, despite the scarring on her side. Dilly breathed in long and hard to regain her breath and strength as she prepared herself to fight. Eight wolves lined up side by side and started to fan out, they intended to attack on all sides.

'You killed Lightning,' snarled Ursa, son of Antares, 'he fell into the river and was swept away, Sasha is torn and bloody. You will pay for this!'

'I killed neither.' Dilly stated bravely, 'You should not have encouraged a young wolf to jump and do the wrong thing. Lightning chose to jump. I forced no one, I killed no one. The fault lies at your feet, not mine.'

'You're unnatural! A freak of nature!' Corvus spat nastily.

The pack steadily approached, heads down, teeth bared. They growled angrily and took their time. They were in no rush; it was obvious that Dilly could not escape.

'Don't like your chances, cub.'

The nonchalant voice came out of nowhere, Dilly jumped, the voice sounded familiar. The wolves became more brazen as they saw Dilly startle and look around, they thought Dilly was showing fear.

Ursa growled, 'There's no escape for you, Dilly. Today, you will experience pain!'

'Nasty piece of work, that one,' the voice came again, *'eight to one, even I consider that unfair.'*

Dilly shivered, she thought she recognised the voice. Now she had eight wolves and Primrose to deal with.

Primrose had been out in the forest, testing the Invisibility and Barrier Spells and had been totally surprised when a young wolf had run straight past her and not even picked up her scent. It pleased her to know that her magic was getting stronger. She was even more surprised to realise that she knew the fleeing wolf. Believing it would be an ideal opportunity to practise another new spell, Primrose decided to practise the sending and receiving of unspoken thoughts.

'Relax, Dilly. They can't hurt you and neither will I. They can't hear me either, only you can. I can also read minds. They don't like you very much,' Primrose laughed, *'Didn't think you would recognise me so quickly.'*

Dilly thought she heard Primrose laugh and wondered why she would do that? She was confused. Why couldn't she see her? Where was she?

'Magic,' Primrose remarked or rather sent her thoughts to Dilly, *'I'm becoming quite good at it. How about we give those wolves the fright of their lives?'*

'Sounds good to me, but how?' Dilly thought, her survival instinct kicking in. She was unsure whether Primrose was being truthful. She feared that Primrose could still hurt her, but she was also acutely aware that without her help, she would not survive this fight.

'I told you, I'll not hurt you. I meant it. Do as I say and say what I do,' Primrose added seriously, wanting Dilly to trust her. Primrose was beginning to enjoy herself immensely. The situation also had an added bonus - testing her magic for real. Dilly's insecurities and the pack's lust for revenge would test her developing skills perfectly.

The pack had stopped. Dilly seemed preoccupied and not at all worried at their approach. Thinking that Dilly did indeed have magic, the first wave of doubt swept through the pack. They believed Dilly should be preparing to fight, but she stood motionless.

Dilly heard Primrose give out an infectious laugh as she picked up on the pack's confusion,

'Oh, funny, very funny, they think you have magic, Dilly. How on earth did you manage to convince them of that?'

'I didn't, you did!' Dilly thought.

'But I don't know them,' Primrose queried; her curiosity piqued.

'They've heard stories about you and they think I should be dead, because of the wound you gave me!' Dilly couldn't help it, but she found she couldn't keep the hurt and anger out of her thoughts, especially when it came to her disfigurement.

'Now, now, Dilly, play nice… show me!'

'How can I? I don't know where you are!'

Primrose laughed again, *'Good point, I forgot. Let's wind the pack up a bit, turn your back on them. Don't worry, they can't hurt you. Trust me!'* Primrose repeated as Dilly faltered.

Primrose became serious for a moment, it had been such a long time since someone had trusted her and she was surprised to realise how much she wanted Dilly to.

'Trust you! After what you did to Briony and Elina,' Dilly almost screamed, but nevertheless, she did as she was asked.

'I cannot change what happened that day,' Primrose added with a tinge of regret. She then became quiet as she surveyed the damage done to Dilly's side.

'I did that!' Primrose was stunned and felt a flicker of guilt, no wonder Dilly was having trust issues. *'Who healed you?'*

'Elina.'

Primrose knew for a fact that Elina could not have healed that wound. She was too inexperienced and most of her magic had been drained when she herself had been restored to life. It might have been possible for Elina to ease the pain but nothing more - Primrose's reading of the Ancient Tome had taught her that. So, that meant one thing - the only people with enough experience to heal a wound like that was Briony or worse still, Vile Vi.

As Dilly turned to face the pack again, she was surprised that they had not moved; they were just staring at her, confused and wary. They could not understand Dilly's behaviour; no wolf in their right mind would turn their back on their enemy.

'Warn them off, Dilly, tell them to go, use your own words. Their indecisiveness is beginning to bore me.'

Dilly recognised the change in Primrose's voice and mood, but again, she did as she was told.

'You all need to turn around and go. If you stay, I will be forced to use magic and it won't be pleasant.' Dilly spoke with confidence and authority.

'That'll be interesting to see you use magic,' Primrose thought with amusement.

'I won't need to, you said I was safe and to trust you, so I know you will,' Dilly thought, with a smirk.

'Clever girl, I like it, testing me!'

The wolves faltered. Dilly gave a sudden pounce forward and was amazed to see all of them jump back quickly.

'Go! I won't say it again!' Dilly threatened.

But still the wolves refused to move, either forwards or backwards.

Primrose sent another thought to Dilly, *'Dilly, turn your bad side to them and say, "If I can do this to myself, think what I can do to you!"'*

Dilly did not falter, if Primrose was about to do what she believed had been impossible, she was not going to give her an opportunity to change her mind. With a clear, strong, confident voice Dilly repeated the phrase and at the same time showed the wolves her disfigured side. Dilly felt a soft touch on her head, while another hand gently stroked the scar.

The wolves couldn't believe their eyes, in front of them Dilly's scar completely disappeared; fur grew and matched the pattern identically to the other side. Dilly was totally healed - the wolves were stunned and shocked. They paled visibly.

They turned tail and fled; one-hundred percent convinced that Dilly possessed magic. They were dreadfully panicked and frightened, finally believing that Dilly was capable of doing them untold harm. Not one of the wolves had the sense to ask themselves why Dilly had not healed herself sooner and avoided all of her suffering.

Dilly collapsed thankfully onto the ground.

Laughing so much that she was fit to burst, Primrose stepped forward and her cloak slipped momentarily to reveal a near spitting image of Elina. The only difference being the short, golden hair. Gone was everything that had been grey. Gone was the monstrosity of a stone foot. Primrose was normal and so, so pretty. Dilly was amazed.

'Close your mouth, Dilly, it doesn't suit you gawping like that,' Primrose said with amusement, quickly adjusting the cloak and hoping Dilly was now within her invisibility barrier, 'Come, let's go home.'

Dilly, without question, rose to her feet and started to walk by Primrose's side, totally besotted. Every now and then, she would stop and turn around to make sure that the scar had truly, truly gone.

It reminded Primrose of the time her foot had become normal again. She knew exactly how Dilly felt.

Walking inside her barrier spell, Primrose and Dilly completely disappeared from view. Primrose could not help but trail her fingers on top of Dilly's head and occasionally scratch her between the ears. She remembered the time when a baby otter had nestled against her and of the comfort she had received from it. Primrose felt she had made a friend, an ally. She smiled; the smile was brighter than the sun.

7. JACK RECEIVES A MESSAGE

Jack paused from his fruitless search. He did not know how it had happened, but he had lost something important. The last time he had seen it was on the night of the Full Moon during the meeting at the fallen oak tree - Primrose's scarf had disappeared.

Jack had left Velvet and Victor to continue their search for Primrose. He, on the other hand, needed to retrace his steps carefully. Every place of rest and every room in the cottage had been meticulously searched, as well as every forest trail they had visited, but no luck. The scarf had gone. Jack knew that many animals had seen that scarf and any one of them could have taken it; there had been much jealousy, some had thought Primrose did not deserve such a gift.

Jack felt he had failed totally. It had been almost two weeks and along with the disappearance of Primrose's scarf there had also been no news of Evelyn. Briony's voice seemed to whisper in his ear, 'everything will be fine, remember don't give up,' but Jack couldn't help feeling depressed, surely things couldn't get any worse.

'*Oh, things could get worse, a lot worse,*' an ethereal voice floated on the air and then wafted away gently into the dimming light.

Jack shook his head, hearing voices now, he thought. He knew he must get some sleep soon or he would go mad. Perhaps he had done that already, he smirked at that idea.

A faint howl drifted through the air. Jack's smirk widened: he was definitely going mad. As the howl continued, Jack recognised the familiar sound, a coded message and a request for help from Orion, a wolf and his dear friend. The message required his surgical skill; a wolf had been injured in a deep gully. Orion was asking him to travel to a certain position, just inside the Ancient Forest on the northern side of the island.

Jack, who had once tended the forest in that area, knew the place Orion referred to straight away. He stood, cupped his hands to his mouth and howled his answer, just as Orion had taught him. He hoped that his answer would travel the distance through the still night's air and be received.

Gathering up his rucksack, Jack started on his way. He was aware it would take him most of the night due to the distance and his leg, which was becoming more and more painful as the days passed. Sleep would have to wait for another night.

As Jack followed the forest trails, he recalled the events since his wife's funeral. He was relieved that he would be seeing Orion soon. His friend's advice and company were important to him and there were some unsettling things that had happened recently that needed to be discussed. He wanted Orion's point of view and to mull everything over with him.

One of the things that concerned him was Bolter the rabbit, who was becoming extremely worried. Strange messages had been intercepted that were causing confusion and anxiety, as well as a lot of misunderstandings; these messages had not originated from his warren. As a result, Bolter and Jack had devised a new secret code; they would now be able to distinguish which messages were true or false.

The rabbits had also noticed strange things flying in the sky. Things that looked like birds but weren't. Jack had yet to see one of these contraptions and wondered what their purpose might be.

Jack's mind went back to the missing scarf again; he felt certain that it had been stolen at the meeting and felt sure the irritating robin was the culprit. The robin had continually interrupted the meeting at the fallen oak tree and didn't like the idea of Primrose having the scarf, but without any evidence Jack was unable to accuse him of the theft without causing animosity.

Then there was that strange voice that Jack thought he had heard earlier, he wondered whether he should mention that to Orion too.

He glanced at the Ancient Tree as he passed it, remembering old times. Even the Tree looked different tonight, better somehow, less threatening. It was hard to see what was different, though, as the night cast too many dark shadows.

The final and most unsettling thing that had happened, to which Jack had no reasonable explanation - was that Briony's coffin had vanished. Around the empty, granite plinth four roses had grown miraculously, each one was heavy with many wonderful, exotic blooms and although, only one primrose had been planted, they had spread like wildfire and carpeted the glade entirely.

The vivid, vibrant colours of the primroses complimented each rose perfectly. Jack could not make head or tail of it. It was a beautiful sight, breathtakingly so, but could it be a sign that Primrose was becoming a powerful magician? Or was it Briony's way of saying that everything was as it should be?

Jack could not wait to see Orion again.

8. ELINA AND VIOLETTE

Elina was sitting by herself at the computer desk in Primrose's bedroom. Violette had just left. Violette was looking after Elina while she recovered from Primrose's attack. Elina was feeling much stronger now, Violette's cooking and tonics had done her a world of good, but Elina missed her father, Jack, and wished to be back in the forest.

During the past week or so, Elina and Violette had both settled into a comfortable routine. Elina spent the mornings with Shadow, formerly known as Trouble, walking to the outskirts of a nearby wood or to the local park. People often stared at the strange, pale girl with the growing wolf cub that Elina passed off as a German Shepherd dog. She was surprised that they believed her and by how gullible some of them were.

While she spent time with Shadow, Violette baked high quality cakes for all occasions in her pristine modern kitchen with all the mod cons. She then delivered them to her own delicatessen called, 'Cakes to Die For'. Elina had thought it was rather an unusual name, but looking at the finished articles - beautifully decorated, adorned to perfection to suit all occasions, maybe it was not such a weird name after all.

The cakes were true masterpieces which smelled and tasted

divine - according to the reviews Elina had read online. Even the other delicacies made on the shop's premises received high praise: 'never tasted anything so scrumptious', 'a feast for the eyes as well as the stomach', 'melt in the mouth loveliness', 'pastries that take you to heaven'. Elina couldn't find any bad reviews concerning her aunt's business.

There were just two, additional house rules that her aunt had insisted on: Elina was never to enter the kitchen whilst her aunt was cooking and never, ever to enter her bedroom without an invitation. Elina was more than happy to follow these stipulations, although she was slightly concerned by just how many more secrets her aunt kept from her. She also found it strange that her nose had never savoured the delicious smell of home-baking like it had done at the cottage. Then again, her aunt's kitchen was always immaculate within seconds after every baking session. Elina was certain that was due to magic, magic that Violette tried hard to keep hidden from her.

Elina's hands were poised over the keyboard of Primrose's computer. Violette had given her one quick lesson on how to use it, but at times she was still baffled by all the things it allowed her to do. She had finally discovered the game Primrose loved to play, which involved the hunting, stalking and capturing of various animals through different landscapes, resulting in their eventual slaughter.

The more difficult the hunt and intricate the capture the more points, strength and levels Primrose's character gained. However, although Elina was shocked at the cruelty portrayed in the game, it was not that, that had momentarily confused her, but a red icon that had just popped up on the screen as she'd opened the game. The icon demanded her attention and informed her that immediate action was required. Many urgent notifications had been received and now, at this moment in time, Elina was unsure whether to acknowledge the messages or not.

Violette had warned her that clicking on unknown pop-ups could infect the computer with viruses that could cause all sorts of problems. She did not particularly want to upset Violette and create a scene. Her aunt was somewhat unpredictable, extremely nice one moment and snappy the next. So, as her fingers lingered over the red icon, she debated whether or not to take the risk.

Elina had learnt very quickly to keep on her aunt's good side and give her a wide berth when one of her moods descended on her. She smiled as she remembered the first time she had called Violette 'aunt' and the momentous reaction it had caused. Violette had been surprisingly angry; she was never, ever to be called aunt, as it made her appear to be old. If anyone was to ask, Elina was to say Violette was a good family friend and she was staying with her until her father was well enough for her to return home. Elina was to call her Violette at all times.

Elina thought that Violette had a huge hang up about her age and looks, but this was not so. Elina was unaware of the many dangers Violette was trying to protect her from. Violette was trying hard to obscure any family connection. She did not want anyone to know that Elina had the possibility of possessing magic.

As the arrow hovered over the red icon, Elina made the decision and pressed the button on the mouse. Violette was out, so what harm could come from her innocent curiosity? A message popped up immediately.

Darius:
Primrose, please message me!
Need HELP!!!
Running out of time!
PLEASE!!!!!!!

After reading the message Elina noticed there were several more; she scrolled back through the history and was amazed at how many messages had been received, all unanswered. Every message asked her to get in touch or demanded to know where his gaming partner had got to and what had he done to upset her?

Elina noticed there was a space for her to type an answer and began to wish she had not clicked on the icon, when another message popped up on the screen.

Darius:
Message me!
Where have you been?

Hearing a noise, Elina looked over her shoulder and listened carefully but heard nothing more. She laughed at herself, she realised she was feeling a little bit guilty and wondered why. It was not as if she was doing anything wrong, surely? Elina came to a decision, she began to type an answer.

Primrose:
She's not here. She's missing.

Darius:
Missing! Where? When?
Who are you?

Now, how to answer that one, Elina wondered. She could not really explain that her mother had turned Primrose into stone for many years and then she herself had freed her with magic, magic that she had not even realised she possessed. That explanation was far too long and was not very credible either. So she decided to be a bit liberal with the truth.

Primrose:
She was unwell for a long time
and then she just disappeared.

Darius:
Not good! Not good at all!
She's in trouble.
You're all in trouble.
You need to...

Elina jumped, she heard another noise in the corridor, just outside her door; Violette had come back unexpectedly. Glancing quickly back at the screen, she noticed the message was a bit longer, but only just had time to read the last few words as her door opened.

... at the Ancient Tree in the forest.

Violette's voice called sharply from the entrance of the room and her eyes fixed onto the screen, an intense wave of concentration flickered across Violette's face, 'What are you doing? That's not the game! Who are you messaging?'

Elina was surprised at the steely tone in her aunt's voice. She turned towards her and the glare she received startled her even more.

'I clicked on a red icon and this all came up, someone called Darius wants to speak to…'

Violette paled visibly, she charged across the room, muttered something forcefully but indistinguishable under her breath and then pushed Elina roughly and violently off the chair, without a thought for her safety. Elina stumbled, hit her head on the edge of the computer desk and fell to the floor.

Violette did not notice, she was completely oblivious of her actions towards Elina and appeared not to care. She quickly scanned the last message and turned off the screen, before snatching the plug from the wall, ending all communications abruptly.

It was then Violette looked around and for a moment looked stunned to see Elina crumpled on the floor rubbing her head. She stretched out a hand towards her and then withdrew it; a moment of confusion floated across her face. Violette bit her lip, flinched as though in pain, her eyes glistened and just as quickly she gained control of herself again.

'Sorry, Elina, but I just lost it a bit there. That man…' Elina noticed that her aunt was shaking. She looked really shocked, 'that man! He kept on at Primrose. It was all very upsetting.' Violette paused.

Violette then went on to explain how Darius had tried to gain Primrose's trust and goodwill in order to set up a meeting with her and how dangerous that could have been; especially when you have no idea what a person was like. Violette told Elina that it had all began when Primrose had started playing that awful game. Darius had managed to gain her daughter's trust and how lucky it had been that she had discovered the messages. She had given Primrose a stern lecture concerning the dangers of speaking to strangers on the internet.

Primrose had not taken her mother's advice at all well and from that day onwards Primrose had become more troublesome, and that was another reason why she had sent her to Briony's that day, long ago. Primrose had not appreciated her mother going through her things.

Elina listened to her aunt's explanation, but there was something about her manner that seemed wrong. Violette refused to look her in the eye. Not once did she offer to help her up from the floor or ask about her head, which Elina knew was bleeding slightly. Something definitely did not seem quite right: Violette was definitely hiding something or lying!

'So you see, I was so concerned for your safety, I had to act quickly. He's a bad man, Elina, a dangerous man. In fact, I don't think you should go on the computer again, at least, not until I have checked it out thoroughly. I have to keep you safe. Jack would not forgive me if something was to happen to you. Let me put a cold compress on your head. It was such a shock to me. It was like all that trouble I suffered with Primrose was happening to me again. Please forgive me.'

As Violette saw to the cut on Elina's head she suddenly lowered her voice and asked, 'Did you read the last message?'

'Yes, he said we are all in trouble. Is that true?'

'It's just a way to get you to feel sorry for him, he is trying to persuade you to meet him and then…' Violette visibly shuddered, '… I hate to think what would happen to you then. Did you read anything else?'

'No,' Elina replied, 'was there something more? I looked around and saw you and then you…'

'I'm so sorry about that, that was wrong of me, but I was so scared for you. Forgive me?'

Elina nodded, she was not sure why she did not tell Violette about the last few words, but for now she wanted to keep them to herself. Something still struck her as odd, even suspicious concerning her aunt's behaviour. Elina could not understand why she continued to be unsettled by her aunt.

From down below a howl could be heard; Shadow's signal that he had returned and was ready to come up to the apartment. Elina grabbed her coat and excused herself from her aunt and silently welcomed Shadow's timely interruption.

When she reached the door to the apartment, she noticed Violette had followed her; she turned and faced her aunt and said quietly, 'Thank you for keeping me safe, but please don't push me like that again. Shadow won't like it either.'

Elina quietly shut the door and went to meet Shadow. Shadow, was unaware that he was about to get another walk. Elina had a lot to think about.

Violette watched Elina leave; her life had just become even more complicated. She had hated lying to Elina. Darius should have been dead; he had died on the night of the Great Flood by her hand or so she had been led to believe. Now, she had no idea what should be done about this new development.

Twenty-five years ago, she had asked Nastarana to check on Darius, her husband, and he had confirmed to her that he was indeed dead. So now Violette was extremely angry. She could not stop shaking. Either Nastarana had not told her the truth all those years ago or he had just managed to message Elina? Either outcome was unacceptable and dreadful to contemplate. Could Nastarana have been so cruel as to keep Darius alive and torment him for that amount of time? Just how much trouble were she and Elina in now? The tight-rope that Violette walked upon had just been given a forcible yank; her world wobbled dreadfully.

Violette knew she was being watched extremely carefully and had no way of visiting the Ancient Tree without increasing the suspicions or wrath of Nastarana. Violette needed to think very carefully about her next step; too many lives depended on it.

9. ELINA COMES TO A DECISION

Shadow lay hidden in a small garden opposite Violette's apartment and watched the thickened glass door of the apartment building; he expected to see Elina at any second. He spotted her walking slowly across the marble-floored foyer. She seemed subdued to him and deep in thought. As she crossed the road towards him, he noticed a mark on her head and smelled a trace of blood. A low growl vibrated in his throat; he was instantly alert. He saw her raise her right hand, Shadow stood and watched. Elina pointed away from the apartment.

Shadow realised he was staying out for longer and was pleased. He was not keen on their new home and longed for the variety of smells and colours of the forest. Elina quietly signalled for him to turn off the main road. He found this strange as they did not usually go in this direction, especially when it would be dark soon - he hoped they were heading to the city park.

He felt Elina's hand stroke his head. He knew that whatever bothered her was nothing to do with him. This was her way of telling him that everything was fine and he raised his head against her hand in acknowledgement. They continued on together along the quiet residential road in a comfortable silence. The path would lead to an ornate iron gateway, the entrance to the park.

Elina sat down on a bench under a tree, out of sight of the road and just inside the park.

'I need to think for a while, Shadow. Feel free to explore, but don't go too far,' she said, speaking softly.

For a moment Elina watched a large bat glide and swoop oddly along the edge of the trees. She felt sorry for it, as it seemed to have something wrong with one of its wings. She noticed that on some of its turns it had a tendency to jerk slightly. She felt odd too, sort of broken like the bat, so much had happened since her mother had died.

Shadow watched Elina for a while and although he could sense she was troubled, he was also sure that she was in need of some quiet reflection. He left her side, but was determined to keep her in sight, feeling sure Violette was the reason behind Elina's uneasiness. He too had noticed the bat and thought it odd, he also noticed a fox slink off into the bushes nearby. The fox was no threat to him and he did not give chase, but he was pleased to see the bat disappear, something was not quite right with it.

Scratching vigorously at his healing wounds, Shadow had some of his own quiet reflections concerning his first encounter with the neighbourhood dog pack. They had assumed that they could take advantage of his youth and inexperience and had tried to run him off their patch, believing him to be an easy target.

Six dogs had surrounded him on his first solo foray; they thought he should be taught a lesson. At the beginning it was an uneven fight, but Shadow had been underestimated. He had learnt some valuable lessons the day Elina had discovered she had magic. Living wild in the forest had given him strength, stamina and speed. His play fights with Dilly and Junior had also taught him many defensive skills. These skills had come in handy during that fight. Even Victor would have been proud of the height of some of his jumps.

Shadow remembered how he had perfected his hunting and stalking skills to track down each of those dogs. He had used darkness as a cover and the element of surprise, each of them received an unpleasant one-to-one encounter. Now they gave him a wide berth, always wary and scared. Shadow had become a silent, invisible presence and at times he still enjoyed making them jump by testing his stealth skills. Shadow was no longer the bumbling cub he once used to be.

Elina stood up and wrapped her coat round herself more tightly; she had become chilled by sitting still for so long. Shadow was at her side immediately and rubbed himself up against her legs. She bent down, placed her head alongside his and hugged him tightly for a moment.

'Tonight, Shadow, we go home,' she stated quietly.

Shadow could not contain his excitement, he jumped up and placed his paws on Elina's shoulders and licked her face madly with his rough tongue, and Elina laughed.

'I hadn't realised how big you've grown, steady boy or you'll knock me over. Do you think you can find the way back to the cottage? I'm not telling Violette. We'll leave as soon as she falls asleep.'

'I know the way even with my eyes closed,' Shadow replied happily.

'That won't be necessary,' Elina grinned, 'but you could use that excellent nose of yours to show us the way.'

'What happened?' Shadow asked with concern.

'That doesn't matter now, but my aunt's behaviour is weird, she's acting too oddly for my liking. I don't trust her.'

'Let's go now then,' Shadow suggested eagerly.

'There's something I need to do first and she will be waiting for me tonight. Once she's asleep and I have reassured her, we'll go. Come let's go back, it's getting dark. Shadow, I need you to stay by my side tonight, especially if she's in the room with me. Something's not right and I know between the pair of us we'll sense if something strange is going to happen.'

10. VIOLETTE'S BEHAVIOUR CAUSES CONCERN

L
ater that night, Elina heard a soft, hesitant knock on her bedroom door, which in itself was strange, Violette normally entered her room without warning. As Violette stepped into the room, she held before her a delicious looking cream cake, decorated generously with soft, lemon icing - Elina's favourite flavour.

'*I* made a little something for you, to show you how sorry I am,' Violette spoke with concern and contrition, but to Elina's ears her voice seemed somewhat contrived and false, but she held out her hand and accepted the gift.

'It looks beautiful, Violette, thank you.'

'Eat it now... *if you like*,' Violette added after a short pause.

Elina felt a small vibration tingle round her neck from the scarf her mother had made her; she also felt a slight pressure against her leg as Shadow leant into her.

'It looks too good to eat. I'll eat it later, if you don't mind. At the moment I would like to admire it, it will taste all the better for it - waiting awhile. Violette, thank you again, it's beautiful, my favourite colour as well.'

'As you wish, *sleep* well, Elina *dear*. Let me know if you need anything.'

As Violette left the room, she glanced over her shoulder, looked at the cake and then at Elina, 'Let me know *if* you like it. I tried a *new* recipe today.'

When Violette left the room, Elina looked at the cake and turned it round, admiring its beauty; once more she felt a vibration around her neck. The scarf her mother had made her had reacted both times the cake had been touched. Even Shadow stood on his hind legs and tried to move her hands from the tempting delicacy, sniffing it warily.

Elina removed the scarf from around her neck and placed it to her face and breathed in, hoping to bring her mother closer to her and then carefully placed it next to the cake - it seemed to sparkle. Elina knew she would not be eating that cake. Her suspicions concerning Violette deepened and it was not just because she had called her 'dear' for the first time. Magic was definitely in the air. Not only that, but she wondered why Violette had stressed certain words, it was not like her. She also never tried new recipes. Her cakes were delicious enough.

When Elina was sure Violette wouldn't be coming back, she ran her hands softly against the underside of the computer desk, at which she sat. Earlier when she had fallen, she had noticed something had been taped there. Elina was determined to retrieve whatever it was. Secretly and carefully, Elina removed the tape and let the item drop into her skirt and remain hidden within its folds, just in case she was somehow being watched. For a brief moment, she wondered where all this paranoia was coming from.

Elina refused to switch on any lights and as her room

darkened she pretended to watch the town's nightlife awaken through her balcony window. When she considered it to be dark enough, she picked up the cake and pretended to eat it. She was not happy with all this subterfuge, but she considered it to be vitally important.

Finally, she knocked on her aunt's bedroom door and opened it, not waiting for an answer.

Violette was sitting at her dressing table, facing the mirror. From the doorway Elina was startled to see that the reflection in the mirror showed a strangely, haggard face with red-rimmed eyes and puffy cheeks, an old face. Elina felt she sensed another tortured soul like she had with Primrose on that fateful day her mother had died. Her aunt was always immaculately presented; the face she saw in the mirror was so unlike her. Elina was about to offer comfort, but she saw something glint in Violette's eyes and her scarf tingled unpleasantly - a warning. She said nothing.

Violette swept her hand between her face and the mirror, her appearance changed instantly - immaculate Violette was back again.

Elina's scarf stopped tingling and she saw Violette take a deep breath. Whatever danger the scarf had sensed had disappeared. It also proved to Elina that she had made the right decision to leave that night.

'I wanted to say that the cake was delicious, the best I've ever tasted, thank you,' Elina lied. It was then she noticed a fine tissue covered bundle next to one of Violette's hands.

Violette also noticed Elina glance at the package and gingerly moved it away with one finger. It was as though she did not want to touch it.

As it moved Elina also saw a silver bracelet, similar to the one Luna had found near her mother's coffin.

'I'm glad you enjoyed the cake, Elina,' Violette said, staring intently at Elina, 'Once again I would like to say how sorry I am. I never meant to hurt you.'

'That doesn't matter now, I know you didn't mean to hurt me,' Elina said softly. As she turned to leave, she needed to ask her aunt one final question, she was curious to know why Violette did not wear the gift that her mother had made her. She knew it was hidden inside the tissue's folds, 'Why don't you wear the scarf?'

A sudden flicker of intense emotion crossed Violette's face as she fought some kind of inner battle and struggled to maintain an element of calmness.

'It's too fine, Elina. I don't want to damage it.'

'But...'

'I said it is *too* fine,' Violette almost snapped, '*Go*, Elina,' Violette smiled slightly and her tone softened, '*leave*...!'

Elina felt that Violette had also added something under her breath, which she could not quite hear, but it heightened her sense of unease.

'You're right, Violette, I do feel as though I could sleep now. For some unknown reason I feel very tired,' Elina lied again and turned slowly to leave the room, but not before she had seen an enigmatic smile tug at her aunt's lips. Violette was definitely acting strangely tonight.

Violette took a deep breath, she knew Elina had not eaten the cake and she hoped that she was also smart enough to have taken the hint to leave, not just her room, but the city! Elina's presence at her apartment and her identity was under suspicion and her sudden entrance into Violette's room had caused an unwelcome visitor to teleport quickly away.

As promised, Shadow and Elina left the apartment building in the dead of night and kept to the shadows as much as possible; two furtive, silent figures making their way back to the people and the place they loved. Neither one had any regrets at leaving Violette or her world behind them. As they made progress and neared the forest, their worries and anxieties lessened, their moods improved and their steps became lighter.

So far, during their escape, they had only been spotted by one animal. Many had been seen, but Elina and Shadow had tried to remain hidden and unnoticed as much as possible.

That one animal had nearly been their undoing. Shadow, on exiting the apartment building nearly placed one of his front paws on a brown rat with black, beady eyes. The surprise for both the wolf and the brown rat would have been hilarious to watch, if speed and silence had not been so pressing.

Both animals had jumped back. Shadow's first instinct had been to chase it. The rat remained motionless and stared at the pair of them, without a concern in the world. Elina placed a gentle hand on Shadow's neck and steered him away from the rat and walked on. However, she could not help but glance back and felt mystified upon seeing that the rat was standing still and watching her.

The rat seemed to smile and the scarf around Elina's neck seemed to hug her warmly. Shadow nuzzled her leg; it was time to move on and the moment passed.

With only a few hours of darkness left, Elina and Shadow

arrived at the outskirts of the Ancient Forest. Passing a litter bin, Elina pulled from her pocket a food bag containing the uneaten cake and dropped the blackened, rotting, gooey mess into it. Elina realised sadly her suspicions had been correct - Violette had tried to poison her.

Still wishing to put as much distance as possible between them and Violette, they hurried on. They kept to the thickest parts of the forests. As Elina walked, she felt another package knock against her legs and wondered what it was that Primrose had felt so important to hide from her mother - she would find out later.

A fox slunk out of the shadows, as soon as Elina and Shadow entered the forest. Softly, it jumped onto the rubbish bin, sniffed inside and grabbed the discarded food bag that had just been dumped. Holding the bag securely between its teeth, it silently disappeared back into the bushes.

11. DAWN LEARNS HOW TO TRUST

As light started to filter across the horizon, Elina rested for a while. She had never walked so far or for so long or in such darkness. Shadow had been her eyes and ears. With no moonlight to guide them Elina would have been lost within a few minutes of entering the forest. Her friend had not grumbled once as she had held onto the scruff of his neck and stumbled many times.

Now, as she trailed her aching, tired feet in the cold waters of the Forest Lake and watched the dawn gradually lighten the sky, Shadow lay at her feet. His flanks rose rhythmically as he slept peacefully and emitted the occasional, soft snore. Elina would sleep later. At the moment, she wanted to enjoy the sights and sounds of the wakening forest, especially welcome after her stay in the city.

Elina spotted an owl gliding silently along the lake's shore. She assumed it was hunting. She was taken by surprise when the owl hovered above her and circled a few times. It seemed to be watching her intently. Suddenly, it swooped down, folded its wings back and landed on a rock next to her without making a sound.

'Hello, Elina,' Dawn hooted.

Elina jumped slightly, Shadow opened an eye, but was soothed back to sleep by a slow and gentle stroke.

'Do I know you?' Elina asked quietly, not wishing to disturb Shadow again.

'Noooo…' Dawn laughed with a hoot, 'I'm Velvet's personal flying machine and I rescued Victor from falling into the river. They are my friends.' Dawn strutted and puffed out her chest, 'I'm a messenger,' she added proudly, 'I deliver messages.' Dawn's dark eyes studied Elina seriously.

Elina leaned back and smiled, she remembered when Velvet had told her he had flown to her mother's funeral and she had not believed him. The thought saddened her. She watched Dawn fluff out her soft feathers; the bird was incredibly beautiful. The mixture of reds, oranges, browns and creams blended with flecks of black made this owl a truly remarkable bird. Elina recognised it as a tawny owl.

'And what messages do you carry and for whom?' she asked. Despite Dawn's claim of knowing her two friends, she couldn't help but feel suspicious. Too much had been happening to her lately, and although her scarf had given her no warning, she knew she had to be careful of who to trust.

'I carry messages between the committee members of the Fallen Oak,' Dawn said with pride and flair.

'And have you got a name? An important messenger must have a name.'

'My name is Dawn, that's the time when I took Velvet for his first flight. Velvet named me - I'm his friend. I'm looking for Jack. Have you seen him?'

Elina was startled once more. Dawn was looking for her father; that meant he must be close by.

'My father doesn't usually come this far upstream. What message do you have for him? You do know he is my father, don't you?'

'Oh yes, yes,' Dawn hooted, 'Victor wants me to tell him that they found where Primrose rested and that she's alive. Did you know he has lost Primrose's scarf? That was one boooooutiful scarf,' Dawn informed her.

Elina thought her father must be devastated at the loss of Primrose's scarf. She knew how important it was for him to complete the tasks on her mother's list, believing it could bring her mother back to him, but Elina was not sure if that was possible. Although she hoped that it was; she also thought that even magic must have its limits, and surely it could only do so much.

'Well, you must tell my father I will keep my eyes open for it, and so will Shadow, my tired, young wolf.' Elina nodded towards him and stroked him fondly once more.

'Dawn?' Elina asked softly, 'Do you think you could give my father another message for me? The trouble is, the message is very, very secret and I don't want anyone else to hear it. Can you come closer so I can whisper it to you?'

Elina held out her hand and waited patiently to see if Dawn would fly to her. Dawn's body language altered dramatically, she began to fidget, her eyes darted nervously about her, searching for an escape route; she was ready to fly off.

'I promise not to hurt you,' Elina said as gently as possible.

'That's what the Summoner said!' Dawn blurted out quickly and angrily. As she mentioned the Summoner's name, Dawn started to shake uncontrollably. Her past was supposed to be her secret and hers alone, not something to be shared. She did not want her new friends to hate her like her previous captor had.

'Who hurt you, Dawn?' Elina asked tenderly, instantly feeling concerned for her.

'Dooo… doesn't matter,' Dawn stuttered.

'But my message is important, Dawn. My father really needs to hear it.'

Elina kept quiet, allowing Dawn time to calm down.

'Can I trust you, really trust you?' Dawn asked, hoping desperately for another friend.

'You can really, really trust me. See how peacefully Shadow sleeps at my feet. Would he be that relaxed if I was nasty to him? And look, he has no leash or collar, he can go whenever he wishes.'

Dawn stared intently at Shadow, Elina was right; Shadow had no silver chain, no silver clasp, rope or harness. She thought Shadow was an extremely, lucky wolf.

Shadow suddenly whimpered in his sleep and Elina gently stroked him again; Shadow settled calmly once more.

'Promise?' Dawn asked.

'Promise,' Elina replied honestly.

Dawn quietly and effortlessly landed on Elina's outstretched hand. Elina felt the poor bird shake nervously.

'You are so light and beautiful, whoever hurt you must have been crazy. Was it Primrose?'

'Noooo,' Dawn shuddered uncontrollably.

'May I stroke you? It might help calm you too, like Shadow.'

Dawn did not know what to do, she froze, but as she watched Shadow sleeping so calmly, she wished that she could have some of that peace too. With some misgivings, she slowly nodded her head.

Slowly, gently and very, very tenderly Elina brought Dawn closer to her, making no sudden movements. She showed Dawn just one finger and with the gentlest of touches, she placed it on her head and delicately stroked Dawn from her head to her tail. Elina could not believe how soft and fragile the bird felt to her touch. She felt Dawn relax and continued to stroke her ever so gently. How could anyone hurt something so beautiful, she thought?

Dawn could not believe how wonderful and magical that touch felt and began to relax properly for the first time in years.

While Dawn relaxed, Elina was having trouble maintaining her calm. Vivid images of despair, cruelty and violence flooded her mind. Images detailing what Dawn had endured, suffered and seen. Elina removed her finger from Dawn's head and was surprised to see she was sleeping peacefully on her hand.

To make herself more comfortable, Elina placed Dawn on her lap and wrapped her gently but loosely in the scarf her mother had lovingly made her. She hoped its magical properties would soothe Dawn further. It was important to Elina that Dawn trusted her when she woke: she did not want her to feel the least bit threatened.

As both animals slept, Elina pulled the package from her coat pocket that Primrose had hidden under the computer desk. Making sure she did not disturb either Dawn or Shadow, she carefully pulled the item from the plastic bag that protected it.

In her hands, Elina held a book. Its cover was decorated in many coloured and pressed primroses, which had then been tacky-backed carefully to the cover. Elina flicked through the pages to reveal a diary. Primrose's secrets, Primrose's deepest feelings, wishes, desires and life laid bare.

Elina felt to read it would be an invasion of privacy, but they needed to know if Primrose was a threat and a danger to them. If this was true, could it reveal why Primrose had behaved so badly or where she might now be hiding? Elina was unsure whether to read it or not.

As it was, the decision was taken out of her hands, Shadow stretched lazily and began to wake up. Once more the diary was returned to the safety of her pocket.

Shadow slowly stretched his head, moved his head closer to Elina's lap and sniffed tenderly at Dawn. He raised one eye quizzically towards her; Elina shrugged:

'I seem to have a strange way of making animals sleep peacefully,' she said, grinning at Shadow and poking him gently with the tip of one chilly foot. She had not dared to move in case she woke Dawn, and her feet had grown quite cold.

Shadow stretched and then once more settled at Elina's feet, she used his warmth to take the chill from her feet.

'What's up with it? Is it ill? Owls are usually very shy and solitary birds,' Shadow remarked.

'This one is special, she knows our friends. Her name is Dawn and when she wakes she may have some news for us.'

Once Dawn woke and found herself wrapped in one of Briony's special scarves, she could not get over her excitement.

Dawn, with Elina's permission, placed the scarf around her, one way and then another as though she was on a cat-walk in a fashion parade. She then flew with the scarf dangling from her feet; it glimmered as it caught the rays of the rising sun. Elina had not noticed until that moment that miniscule pieces of silver had been laced into her precious gift.

Dawn had never been so happy and carefree. She felt as though a world of troubles and darkness had been lifted from her shoulders, and that her sleep would never be broken by nightmares ever again. But best of all, Elina had trusted her to fly with that special scarf, a true sign of friendship and trust. She knew she had made another truly, remarkable friend.

It was not long before Elina and Shadow were up to date with the tasks assigned to each of their friends, the details of the legends, the news that Orion's parents were alive and that they might be quite close to where they now rested. But the first thing Dawn spoke of was the beautiful scarves that Jack had shown them that night and fervently hoped he had not lost both of them.

As Dawn prepared to leave Elina and Shadow, she turned and suddenly asked, 'When I see you next, can I fly with the scarf again and have another massage?'

'I promise,' Elina said tenderly, 'but you must promise to give my father that message.'

'I will, for you, anything,' Dawn called out as she soared effortlessly and gracefully into the air to start her search for Jack.

'What message was that?' Shadow asked, slightly miffed at their earlier whisperings.

Elina understood his curiosity and had been aware that he was unaccustomed to being left out of her thoughts.

'Sometimes, Shadow, I may need to keep things from you, but this time I will tell you…' Elina bent down and whispered softly into his ear, '…I told her to tell my father not to trust Violette one iota and to let him know we are safe and on our way home.'

Shadow no longer felt a little bit jealous of Dawn and together they left the Forest Lake and followed the river, which would eventually take them past the Ancient Tree and back home to the cottage.

12. BRIONY'S BRACELET

Jack rested; he had made good progress, despite his throbbing leg. He reckoned he was more than half way to the gorge Orion had asked him to go to. He probably had around three more hours of walking to do. Feeling peckish, Jack thought it was time for a rest and a bite to eat. He had found a secluded clearing next to the river. At this point it flowed gently into deep pools before continuing its journey downstream.

Jack rested on an old stump, slipped his rucksack from his shoulders, stretched his muscles and sat down. As he ate his sandwich, he noticed small ripples glistening on the smooth surface of the river, as fish fed and swam lazily in the deep, dark pools.

Jack breathed in deeply, enjoying the peace and quiet. He watched the clouds move slowly across the night's sky and heard the haunting hoot of an owl. He used to love sitting by the river with Briony, watching the moon or the sun rise or fall and listening to the sounds of the forest.

'That's it, my love, keep thinking of all the positive memories,' his wife's voice floated comfortingly on the wind.

As he brushed away a tear, he spotted a brown rat with black, beady eyes looking at him inquisitively. Its nose was twitching eagerly as it smelt the meat inside Jack's sandwich.

'Want some?' Jack asked and threw it a bit of sausage. The rat ate hungrily.

Laughing, Jack went to throw a second piece towards the rat but accidently dropped it on his leg. The rat jumped and promptly landed on his knee. She ate quickly; then sat patiently, expecting more.

'Well bless me, if you aren't a bold one!' Jack laughed again, but continued to share his food. It was strange, but his aching leg felt better, the warmth from the rat eased it slightly.

The rat scrambled up onto Jack's shoulder and looked around intently from her new vantage spot, she seemed to be looking for something. Jack offered the rat another piece of his sausage. The rat leaned eagerly towards it and fell - straight into Jack's shirt pocket.

Jack felt the rat panic, turn and twist quickly, as it tried to find a way out. Finally, he felt the rat's sharp claws find a foothold in his shirt. It poked its head out of the pocket, paused for a moment and then leapt and toppled comically into the long grass before disappearing into a hole. Something glinted brightly as the rat fell, Briony's bracelet had got caught up in the rat's legs.

Moving quickly, Jack was relieved to see that the bracelet had become lodged at the entrance of the hole. Breathing quickly and shaking visibly, Jack picked it up, and held it up in the air for inspection. Comforted to see there was no apparent damage, he returned it to the safety of his shirt pocket.

Hoping that the list was also undamaged, he inspected it next and found it to be intact - the three items that needed completing stood out dimly against the white of the paper. He sighed wearily and once more Briony's voice chided - *'Remember, never give up.'*

Meanwhile, the rat hid silently, shaking in a hole near Jack's feet. She breathed rapidly and tried to calm herself down. She had been nervous at the beginning of this task; humans were so unpredictable and she had been unsure whether Jack would be friendly or not. Most humans hated rats!

As she had fallen to the ground, the weight of the bracelet caught in her claws had made her twist painfully but that had miraculously worked in her favour. It had allowed the bracelet to be partially hidden as she fell and also allowed her a few extra precious seconds without Jack noticing a thing. Now, all that she needed was for Jack to pick up the other bracelet that lay on the ground at his feet. The rat felt her heart beat faster as Jack examined the bracelet he had picked up. She desperately hoped he would not discover the switch. She sighed quietly as he placed it in his pocket, and her relief was enormous.

On the rat's back, in a special pouch, now nestled Briony's bracelet and in Jack's pocket lay another. Once Jack moved, she would be on her way back to her mistress, all of her tasks successfully completed. The rat was exhausted and looked forward to going home. Being close to an owl, two wolf cubs and a human had been hard, dangerous work.

Jack shrugged the rucksack onto his back and started to move. His leg felt much better for the rest. In fact, he puzzled, it felt as good as new and strong enough to walk to Violette's apartment. He had an urgent need to check on his daughter. An unsettling thought had been growing in his mind. What if the legends were true and Darius had pulled Violette into the wave? He did not believe Darius was capable of such a thing, but Violette had been very unpredictable at the time.

Jack's mind was made up, after he had seen Orion, he would definitely visit Violette. He wanted answers and his daughter was coming home.

He hoped to see Dawn; perhaps she could then take a message to Elina quicker than he could walk. At least Orion's troubles were in the same direction.

13. FRIEND OR FOE

Primrose had been studying hard; she had mastered the invisibility spell, but was unsure of how long it would last. Dilly, her first ever friend, gave her a special low vibrating growl when the air around her began to shimmer, a sign that her invisibility was wearing off and she would put the cloak on once more.

When she ventured outside and practised her magic, she still took her yellow cloak, just in case. Primrose knew she had made a lot of enemies.

Today her intention was to return to the glade where she had met Dilly and practice the barrier spell. The open space would allow her to create a small safety shield around her and then she would be able to increase the distance slowly. This way she could gauge how far her magic stretched, the strength of it and check for any flaws in her defence.

A barrier spell was meant for protection: it created an invisible, dome-shaped shield around the spell maker. Primrose had perfected it inside the Ancient Tree, now she had to take the next step and achieve it outdoors. After that she would progress and practise inside the forest, where she would have to learn to weave the barrier around many obstacles, without a single flaw.

Primrose thought the glade would be an ideal spot to practise.

Dilly was to be her attacker and hurl herself or obstacles at her shield. Dilly loved helping Primrose with her magic; she treated it as a game and was just as competitive as her. If Dilly found a flaw, she was rewarded with extra pieces of meat and better still was allowed to stretch out on Primrose's comfortable bed. Primrose wondered where Dilly had disappeared to, she must have discovered an interesting scent and gone off to investigate, but she knew Dilly would not be long.

So, you can imagine Primrose's surprise, when she spotted Elina sitting alone, in the middle of the glade, with a book on her lap that looked very much like her diary. Granted, the book was closed, but that did not stop Primrose from getting angry. This shook her up a bit; she had not felt so angry since the day she had gained her freedom. Her foot suddenly ached. She cursed. Her foot started to stiffen. Primrose shook herself and mentally told herself to breathe calmly. Her foot began to relax as she gained control of her temper and calmed herself down.

Elina had had no intention of taking a rest, but she had seen a kestrel hovering overhead intent on hunting something beneath it. Kestrels were not usually seen in the forest, so Elina sat down and allowed Shadow to wander off while she watched the bird dip and soar several times. Eventually, it flew off without catching anything.

Once more, Elina pulled Primrose's diary from her pocket and traced the delicate primroses on its cover. Suddenly, she felt a frisson of energy travel towards her and her scarf began to vibrate softly against her neck. Magic was definitely around her, somewhere. Without raising her head, she used her senses to locate the spot from whence the energy pulsed. She saw nothing. The tingle she felt around her neck was not like the feeling she had sensed at Violette's apartment; that meant the only other person in the forest that had magic was...

'Hello, Primrose,' Elina remarked, as casually as possible, looking straight at the energy source, acutely aware that she was in the presence of the person who had been instrumental in her mother's death. She was not sure how she should feel towards Primrose at the moment. The shock of meeting her so unexpectedly had caused her mind to go temporarily blank.

Primrose was startled, for a moment she thought her magic had failed, but the cloak was pulled around her and the hood was up, so there was no way Elina could see her.

Elina continued to stare in Primrose's direction. Primrose stared back at her, acutely aware of their last meeting and of the awful events she had set in motion that fateful day. She had also never used her magic to defend herself or hurt another... yet! Primrose was in a quandary, she was unsure what to do next. If Elina still had magic she could be in serious trouble, but at least she should have the advantage, she could not be seen.

Although, Elina could not see Primrose, she knew exactly where she stood, and was surprised just how easily she could read her thoughts. She began to suspect that she might still have some magic herself. The thought no longer frightened her, but gave her comfort. Sensing Primrose's uncertainty and even some regret, Elina knew she had to say something to diffuse the awkward silence that was growing between them, before one of them did something stupid:

'You're right, I can't see you, but you are standing right there...' she said boldly, pointing straight at her, 'at the moment

I mean you no harm, but I can't promise that will always be the case.'

'While you're about it, why don't you tell the whole world I'm here,' Primrose snapped, slightly alarmed and looking all around her. Her mother's warnings were fresh in her mind. She immediately began to tighten her barrier, moving away at the same time.

The resulting crash was inevitable as two lively wolves reuniting after nearly two weeks apart catapulted themselves against the energy of Primrose's strengthening barrier. As they yelped and scrambled to regain their footing, Dilly and Shadow had both girls in hysterics and the awkwardness felt between them lessened.

Elina still laughing rushed towards Shadow to comfort his bruised ego and confusion; his sister, Dilly, had suddenly disappeared inside Primrose's barrier.

'Where's she gone? Where's she gone?' Shadow panicked.

'Shush, Shadow, everything is fine. It looks as though Dilly has found an unlikely friend,' Elina said, trying to comfort him.

'I heard that,' Primrose interrupted, 'what's that pup mean? Why can't he see, Dilly?'

'She's disappeared, she's invisible like you,' Elina answered, 'all I can see is the forest. Everything looks normal, but you and Dilly are both invisible. Shadow, it's fine, Dilly's OK, she's with Primrose.'

Elina was trying hard to calm Shadow down, but he was having none of it and at the mention of Primrose's name, he started to growl fiercely. Shadow was definitely ready for a fight. Elina quickly placed a hand on his head to calm him, 'Send Dilly out, he needs to see her.'

'I've a better idea, send him in and let me know if he disappears too, if he does follow him in,' Primrose ordered seriously, 'it's important.'

Elina bent down to Shadow and met his questioning eyes, slightly annoyed at Primrose's superior and authoritative tone.

'Can we trust her?' he asked.

'Dilly does and I hope we can. The scarf has given me no warnings and mother did make it for me,' Elina tried to reassure him as well as herself. She hoped she was not about to make an awful mistake.

Shadow entered the barrier cautiously, hackles up and ready to fight if necessary and disappeared. Elina nervously followed him in, just as a bat with an odd flight pattern entered the glade.

Dilly's greeting of Elina was exuberant; she now had her most favourite person back in her world and her youngest brother. Turning to Primrose, wagging her tail furiously, she realised that she had been wrong; she actually had two special friends. Dilly was the happiest wolf in the world, but the silence between the girls was deafening, both were unsure of what to do or say next.

In the end it was Elina that broke the silence by holding out Primrose's diary, 'I have not read a word of this diary. I only stayed with your mother for nearly two weeks, and I'm sorry to say, she has to be the most unpredictable person I know. I nicknamed her Vile Vi.' Elina tried hard to be civil and had said the first thing that had entered her head.

Primrose laughed, feeling at last she and Elina had something in common and she took her diary from Elina's hands, 'Same here, but that's not the only name I called her, maybe we can share or invent a few more, but now I really do need as much help as possible to perfect this spell.' Primrose saw Elina stiffen slightly and hastily continued, 'I know we're not going to be the best of friends, but I could seriously do with some help, even if it's only for a little while. I knew I was invisible, but I did not realise until now that I could make others invisible too. I have learnt that there is a bigger threat to everyone, other than myself! So, I would dearly love your help,' she looked down at Shadow, 'yours too, Trouble, if you don't mind.'

'My name is Shadow. I'm not Trouble any more. That was a stupid name,' Shadow growled. He was not prepared to trust Primrose yet. He was feeling rather unsettled, Primrose looked so different, but oddly familiar.

'And what threat would that be?' Elina asked suspiciously. She felt Primrose had an awful lot of explaining to do and felt angry and upset with her.

'I can understand your suspicions of me, truly I do, but this invisibility thing is vitally important, probably even for the both of us. I can explain everything later, but I would dearly love you to trust me... and I'm aware that's a big *ask*!' Primrose replied looking Elina in the eye.

Elina returned Primrose's stare, she felt her sincerity and noted she hid nothing from her. For the moment, she decided to give her the benefit of the doubt and reluctantly agreed to help. She had every intention of talking to her later concerning her mother's death.

By the end of the afternoon, Primrose could not believe the progress that she had made, all thanks to the help of Elina, Dilly and Shadow. Both the invisible and barrier spells were operating much wider and better than Primrose could have ever imagined. Furthermore, the discovery that she could decide what or who could remain invisible within the barrier delighted her no end. They had even been successful in the deeper parts of the forest too and to top it all, Elina and Primrose had actually become slightly more comfortable with each other.

Later, while they rested and sat with Dilly and Shadow, Dilly finally told Elina how she had found Primrose. She told her of the new pack and how they had bullied her until she was forced to run from them. She laughed as she remembered how they had scared the pack into believing she had magic, while Primrose had secretly healed her ugly scar.

Elina then quietly brought Primrose up to date concerning her mother's death, the list and the search for her that was still ongoing. She even told her about her stay with Violette and finished with a description of the poisonous cake. Once she had finished talking, she turned to Primrose and took hold of her hands unexpectedly.

The action surprised both Primrose and herself. Elina, without realising it, was using her magic for the first time. As soon as she touched Primrose's hands, she began to sense some of her grief, sadness and regret. Elina knew Primrose had not lied to her.

'I didn't mean for your mother to die. I wondered why the forest was so quiet the day I found my new home. I wasn't a nice person back then, but I promise Elina that I have changed and her death will not be in vain. I will use my magic for good and never for evil.'

The two girls sat together in silence, both deep in their own thoughts, when Primrose suddenly turned towards Elina, 'Come back with me, stay the night, there's things you need to see and… I think you should read some of my diary, it might help you understand why I was always so… so…' Primrose was having difficulty finding a suitable word, '…angry with everyone, even Briony. It's even on your way home to the cottage.'

'I can sense certain things, by just looking at you, but…'

'Then you definitely need to come. I have a book. It will help you understand your magic and how to use it. Please Lina, please come back with me. Let me show you I have changed.'

Elina smiled at the nickname that Primrose had just used. Lina, she repeated quietly, she quite liked it.

'How about it, Shadow, would you like to spend a bit more time with Dilly?'

The resulting excitement exhibited by both wolves showed clearly where their preference lay. However, although Elina had unexpectedly begun to enjoy Primrose's company that day, she could not help but wonder if she would ever be able to forgive her for her mother's death.

On the way back to the Ancient Tree, Primrose insisted that they all remained inside the protection of the invisible barrier and promised to explain why later. She was convinced that meeting Elina had not been an accident, and that she definitely needed to enlist her help in fighting whatever was looming on the horizon. If only she could get Elina to truly trust and eventually forgive her.

14. A Message from Briony

Primrose gently placed a finger under Elina's chin and closed her gaping mouth. It had popped open when she caught her first glimpse of the Tree, the place in which Primrose said she now lived. As they reached the enormous trunk, Primrose reached into some undergrowth and pulled out some kind of hidden contraption. She then placed her foot into a harness, held onto a rope and disappeared up and into the top-most branches, much to the surprise of both Elina and Shadow. As she glanced upwards, Elina noticed that all but one enormous branch had fresh, green leaves.

Hearing Dilly bark, Elina turned towards her and saw that she wanted them to follow her down the bank to the river.

Elina was amazed at the space she found herself in, she marvelled at the intricate root system that supported this giant tree and enjoyed the quietness it created.

Shadow used his nose to explore the river's edge, his tail wagging with excitement as he investigated all the different smells, while Dilly sat waiting patiently.

Hearing a noise above her head, Elina glanced upwards and saw a stairway slowly descend from a trap door, Primrose's face stared down at her from the inside of the tree:

'Coming up or not?' she called, thrilled at the prospect of showing Elina her amazing home.

Dilly jumped up the stairs immediately, followed by Shadow, who was not willing as yet to let his sister out of his sight. Elina followed more slowly behind them, taking everything in.

Once more, Elina was startled; she quickly grabbed at Primrose's hand as water started to gush noisily from the roots all around her. Elina noticed with some surprise that all their footprints had been obliterated from the riverbank.

'Can't be too careful,' Primrose said with a huge smile, remembering her reaction when she had had heard the water wash away her footsteps for the first time. She pulled Elina into her home.

'What do you think?' she asked, bubbling with excitement, wanting Elina to be as enthralled with the Tree as she was.

Completely shocked into silence, Elina spun round. Brilliantly polished wooden walls surrounded her, beautifully carved furniture decorated with soft velvet cushions beckoned her, fantastically carved murals on panels vied for her attention, a gorgeous chandelier hung from the ceiling and a winding staircase followed the curvature of the trunk. She took it all in but still she saw more.

Finally, Elina stopped turning and stared at a door on the opposite side of the room under the stairway. Her jaw dropped open once more as she pointed at it. A beautiful carving was materialising in front of her eyes on a door. It slowly revealed a tea party with three wolf cubs, Velvet, Victor and a family of rabbits with Briony and Jack looking on, and there on the edge was a 'spot' surrounded by brambles. If this was not magical enough, ancient lettering above the door slowly revealed the name Elina.

Primrose stood and stared just like Elina; she too gaped at the strange phenomenon that was materialising in front of their eyes. Elina grabbed hold of Primrose's hand again and then let it go, not sure if she was being too friendly, too quickly.

'Shall we?' Primrose nodded towards the door, 'Together?'

Elina nodded in agreement and together they approached the door, Elina turned the handle gingerly, unsure what she was about to find.

'This wasn't here before,' Primrose said, 'I don't understand.'

'Maybe the Tree wants me here too,' Elina said, 'Perhaps it wants us to be together. I'm not so sure what to think. What do you think?'

'I think, I will give up thinking, this Tree takes it too seriously,' Primrose laughed. Elina looked confused.

'You think it and the Tree carries it out. You'll see if you decide to stay,' she explained.

Together they opened the door.

In front of them, another stairway spiralled upwards. Together both girls, trailing their fingers on the smooth, polished walls, climbed the stairs to find another room. Against the wall, they saw a four-poster bed hung with lemon, gauzy drapes. A homely duvet with yellow and white hexagons adorned a deep, soft mattress and a thick piled lemon carpet cushioned their feet.

Another set of stairs led to a bathroom with white fixings; once more the wooden floor and walls were polished to a high finish, revealing the real beauty of the Ancient Tree. Thick yellow towels hung on rails and the scent of freesias filled the air - Elina's favourite scent.

'This place continues to amaze me every day,' Primrose said seriously. 'I think the Tree means for you to stay and that you're not meant to return to the cottage. Something or someone could be waiting for you.'

'What or who on earth could possibly be waiting for me?' Elina exclaimed with surprise.

'Vile Vi, possibly. Also, I have a letter you need to read downstairs that might explain things,' Primrose replied.

As they returned to Elina's bedroom, it was Primrose's turn to point. Three items had magically appeared on the bed while they had been upstairs - another Ancient Tome, a letter and a silver bracelet. Elina looked at Primrose, as she gently pushed her towards the bed:

'Read the letter, Lina, meet me downstairs later.'

Elina sat on the bed, she picked up the silver bracelet and placed it on her left hand and admired the pure diamond that was edged in gold. It resembled the rose she had been named after and it was extremely beautiful.

She removed her scarf and was amazed to see how wonderfully they complimented each other. Her hand stretched towards the letter. She recognised her mother's writing and could smell the sweet perfume of roses on the envelope, her mother's favourite perfume. Finally, she turned her eyes towards the Ancient Tome. It was embossed with gold lettering and runes and titled, 'Harnessing the Mind'.

She reached for the letter and opened it with nervous fingers, praying that Primrose was not playing some kind of horrible trick on her.

Elina started to read the letter.

Dearest Daughter,

I love you so much, but I feel so guilty. I should have told you about Primrose and warned you of the magic you might have possessed. What I did to Primrose will weigh heavily on my mind forever. I failed to protect both of you. I was too weak. When I saw you fall to the ground my world collapsed, how could I have not seen the magic growing within you?

Having you was a blessing, a fantastic surprise for both your father and me. You gave us such joy, such happiness, a chance of motherhood and one I felt I did not deserve. It wasn't until my death that I remembered our first tragic loss. Your father and I lost our first child in that horrendous flood many years ago, along with your Aunt Evelyn (my youngest sister), who was looking after you that night. Darius, my brother, also disappeared that night.

Even now, your father doesn't know what became of our child or Evelyn. We believed them to be safe inside the protection of the Ancient Tree.

There is so much I should have told you, but I felt you were too young to believe in the magic that surrounded us, as well as the danger that threatened us back then and now.

All I ever wanted to do was to protect you and keep you safe.

Be on your guard always my love. Let others earn your trust, and be guided by your inner self.

As you know, my memory was lost during the flood, so many important things lost and forgotten and for so long. Fragments of my past returned bit by painful bit, a jigsaw of jumbled pieces, but some are still lost to me.

When Primrose turned up that day, full of anger and contempt,

I believed the Darkness was threatening us once more. I panicked and regretfully took drastic action: I turned her to stone.

Now, I know that Primrose was on the point of 'flaring', her Dark Magic was too strong for her to control, and without the proper guidance, she was unable to control her emotions.

My heart goes out to her, she had so much to deal with and deserved better from Violette and myself. But who am I to criticise? I too, missed your growing magic and your 'flaring' - what sort of a mother was I?

Primrose needed my help that day and my compassion, not an unjustifiable reaction based on the fear of past events.

Oh yes, Elina, my dearest, I am still close by and my memory is being repaired slowly. Some of the things I am learning about myself are coming as a bit of a shock, but know this one important thing, the love I hold for you is endless and we will see each other again and soon. But at present I am forbidden to tell you how or when.

In fact, my mother will be annoyed when she finds out that I have written this to you. She will call it a breach of safety.

If ever you meet Primrose, please ask her to forgive me, tell her I did love her too and that I should have stood up to Violette. I was not strong enough to cope with my fears and the Dark Magic I possessed. Do not be scared of Primrose, I know there is good in her too; all she needs is a good friend.

Be certain that your father and I love you with all our hearts and souls, even to the furthest stars and back.

'Til we meet again ...

P.S. Wear your bracelet at all times for your protection. When you meet your father again, he will answer all of your questions.

Read the Tome from start to finish, no skipping, just like we always shared our books together.

This letter needs to be destroyed or hidden well: rules have been broken: I should not have done this during these dangerous times.

As Elina gently re-folded the letter and returned it to the envelope, she felt the gentlest of kisses on her forehead, just like her mother used to do and the smell of roses intensified. As tears slowly slid down her cheeks, she looked up and spoke to the air around her, 'I love you too. I know you always did what was best for me. Don't feel guilty; just know that I love you to the Milky Way and back again.'

Looking around, Elina breathed in the lingering smell of roses, comforted in the knowledge that somewhere her mother was alive and watching over her, but best of all her mother was also being cared for by those who loved her. Elina had also made an important decision - she would stay with Primrose, she would give her a chance like her mother wanted, but forgiving and trusting her was a different thing altogether.

Returning downstairs to Primrose, Elina's nose caught the appetising aroma of her mother's hearty broth. She placed the letter and the Ancient Tome onto the kitchen table, next to a steaming bowl of broth and a plate of freshly, baked bread. She smiled warmly at Primrose.

'You OK?' Primrose asked.

'I'm OK,' Elina answered, 'but I think you should read this.'

Elina gently pushed her letter across the table to Primrose, while Primrose reached into her pocket and gently pushed her own letter towards Elina.

'On the condition you read mine as well. I discovered it on my first day here. I believe there should be no secrets between us now. It will help us to learn to trust each other. But first we eat because I'm starving, just like those two,' Primrose said nodding at Dilly and Shadow and trying to dispel some of the tension that might still linger between them.

'You did all this?' Elina asked; looking at their meal and the food the wolves were noisily tucking into.

Primrose raised her eyebrows at Elina and chuckled, 'I wish! Do I look like a cook? The Tree did it!' She laughed further as Elina looked dumbfounded.

A wave of suspicion flickered over Elina's face; she had nearly been poisoned once. She was unsure whether to believe Primrose or not.

'Now, now, Lina, you need to at least try and trust me,' Primrose said, pretending to be offended, 'Test it out, think of a food, remember to ask nicely and see what happens.'

In the middle of the table, a huge chocolate gateau appeared with a jug of fresh cream.

'Not bad for a first attempt,' Primrose said approvingly.

'Let's hope it doesn't turn black and gooey,' Elina laughed and then turned serious for a moment, 'And I agree, no secrets.'

As they ate, Primrose described how she had met Orion and Ebony, eluded Victor, slept with otters and eventually found and entered her new home.

'Strange about the brown rat,' Elina said when Primrose finished her tale. 'When I left the apartment, one nearly tripped Shadow up. It was really funny. Shadow didn't know whether to eat it or chase it, but the rat just stared at us, showing no signs of distress. It was such a strange moment that even my scarf seemed to give me a hug.'

It was then that Elina remembered Primrose's scarf, and she removed her scarf from her neck to show her. 'My mother made me this, it warned me when Violette gave me that cake, but it acted differently with the rat and when you were close by. My mother also made you one too, my father was supposed to give it to you, but it has disappeared. Dawn said it was beautiful and she was cross with my father for losing it.'

Primrose was surprisingly touched to know that Briony had made something special for her, especially after the rudeness she had shown her.

'Who's Dawn?' Primrose asked.

'A Tawny owl. She is acting as a messenger between everyone that's out looking for a girl with a stone foot,' Elina grinned at Primrose.

'It would seem that I'm causing quite a bit of trouble. At first, I was so angry at what was done to me; all I wanted to do was disappear and think of ways of punishing everyone. Now, I'm living proof that some of my wishes can come true: I can disappear at will and go anywhere, and no one will ever see me, but my priorities have changed drastically. Even my right foot starts to feel heavy and begins to ache if I decide to do the wrong thing, so I have to be nice, there's no way I want that back!'

Primrose paused for a while, deep in thought, she then continued more seriously, 'I still want you to read some of my diary. It might help you understand what I was like once, and it might help you to trust me,' she added, looking at Elina hopefully.

'Talking about how you were back then, my mother's letter explains why you could have been acting the way you did. Shall we exchange letters?' Elina suggested gently.

After reading the letters both girls looked at each other, confusion written across their faces. They swapped letters and laid them down on the table next to each other.

'The writing is the same…' they both said in unison.

'Who am I?' Primrose cried, 'Does this mean Briony is my mother and Violette, my aunt, or is she something else entirely!'

'Primrose,' Elina said, standing up, and before she knew it she had put her arms around her, to give her some comfort, 'you are, Primrose. That secret drawer you spoke about will only open for you or your mother.'

At first Primrose accepted Elina's attempt to calm her, but then she began to feel a deep sense of confusion and betrayal. She stepped away:

'Perhaps someone is playing with my mind,' she remarked seriously and looked suspiciously at Elina.

'Remember, Primrose, trust has to work both ways,' Elina replied, with a slight edge to her voice. Once more Elina reacted without a thought and placed her hands directly on Primrose's heart, just as she did to the statue on that fateful day not so long ago. Her own heart beat in time with Primrose's.

Next, she placed her hands on both sides of Primrose's head and looked directly into her confused eyes. Elina removed her hands and sat down. She was shaken by what she had seen and felt.

'Well?' Primrose demanded, mystified and suspicious at Elina's behaviour, 'What exactly was the point of all of that?'

'No one's playing with your mind...' Elina replied quietly, but could not quite hide a slight smile, 'there's nothing there.'

'Not the time for joking, Lina,' Primrose returned equally quietly.

'Well, sister, you'd better get used to it.'

'Sisters?'

'Sisters!

Both girls, caught up in the moment, forgot their suspicions and hugged each other tightly. Then embarrassed at their show of emotion, they quickly let each other go. One minute they had been potential enemies and now they might possibly become friends. They laughed awkwardly. Dilly and Shadow picking up on the change in Elina's and Primrose's attitude towards each other began to howl happily, if somewhat out of tune.

'But how, what did you see?' Primrose asked.

'I saw two images and felt one. Violette cast some kind of appearance spell on you whilst you slept in the cradle and then took you from the Tree.'

'And what did you feel?'

'An extremely, strong blood connection. I'm certain we are not cousins, the connection was just too powerful; add that to the image I saw, the letters, the cradle's secret drawer and the welcome the Tree has given to us both... I can only conclude that Violette swapped babies on the night of the flood and that we are... sisters! You are the child that my mother lost all those years ago!'

15. THE BROWN RAT RETURNS HOME

As dawn finally won its battle over the night, the brown rat with the black, beady eyes arrived at Briony's favourite spot and rested a while beside the river. As colour and light were quickly returning to this world and the shadows were disappearing, the rat could not afford to be late. She sat on her back legs, sniffed the air, looked carefully around, and hastened quickly through the primroses to the granite plinth, where the coffin had once lain. The rat disappeared quickly under the roses and gathered the item it had hidden there earlier.

Suddenly, surrounded by a blinding, white light the brown rat felt both comfort and love; her eyes unaccustomed to the brightness blinked rapidly. The rat was not at all scared. She knew she was being scanned, as was the custom. Her body, mind, soul and even the pouch fastened to her back were being meticulously checked, along with the last item she had picked up.

The rat waited patiently for the ritual to be completed. She knew her deeds of the last few weeks were being fully replayed and analysed. If necessary, these would be discussed later. The rat relaxed, glad to be home.

Home was a safe place, a sanctum for the peaceful souls of

five ghosts and one human. A great injustice had been done to two magicians and their two friends many years ago at the hands of the greatest wizard ever to have lived. Since then, they had been banished, as ghosts, to an underworld home called the Sanctum. A human child, now grown, had arrived on the night of the Great Flood and more recently another ghost had arrived on the night of the last Full Moon.

The soft voice of Forrestiana, the oldest female soul, floated in the air, 'You may fetch your familiar, Sweet Briar; the scan has been completed.'

No footsteps sounded as Briony approached the rat. The gentle swish of a long, white dress swept the white, marble floor and an old soul bent down to retrieve the brown rat, her familiar. All magicians had a familiar, an animal that chose to stay and help them with tasks; familiars could also leave whenever they wished. They were allowed to have free choice.

The rat looked adoringly into the bright eyes of Briony, her ethereal form shimmered in the soft candlelight and her beautiful face was framed by a mass of ghostly, shiny curls; her eyes twinkled merrily at her. To the rat, she was the kindest, most beautiful, magical being in the whole world.

In this world, a soul may be old but outwardly could appear as young as they wished.

'You did well, Sharna, everyone is pleased,' Briony said gently, 'now, let's get you more comfortable.'

Briony took the package from Sharna's mouth and undid the pouch from her back. She was amazed to see that Sharna's teeth had not torn the fine tissue paper that covered Primrose's scarf. Next, she retrieved the bracelet from the pouch and held it to the light and smiled. She had thought it had been lost to her forever.

A soft kiss was placed on the rat's head.

As Briony was about to place the pouch in her pocket, she noticed something else glint within its folds - a small, silver clasp!

Resting on Briony's shoulders, Sharna spoke, 'I found it at the base of the Ancient Tree and thought it might be of some significance.'

'You were right to bring it, Sharna, the markings are familiar, but my memory fails me - my mother, though, will have knowledge of its creator.'

Briony walked soundlessly along a white marble corridor lined with pedestals that were topped with cut crystal vases filled with bouquets of sweet-smelling roses. The rat felt her nose tickle with the heady perfume but knew the sensation would cease as soon as they entered the Hall.

Their way was lit by perfumed candles that flickered happily on silver etched sconces; Sharna's head started to swim. Briony passed her hand gently across Sharna's body and the feeling was gone. The rat had not said a word concerning her discomfort. Sharna rubbed her head against Briony's neck, her way of saying thank you.

Thirteen chairs were positioned around the outer edge of a large circle in the middle of the Great Hall. The circle was known as the Circlet and possessed great magic. The circumference was decorated richly with ancient Celtic symbols and each chair stood in a magical circle of its own. In the middle of the Circlet was another ornate circle, from which radiated lines to each of the thirteen chairs. Inside that inner circle stood an old oak table upon which a solitary red cushion rested.

Each dark oak chair was ornately carved in various designs, four of which were occupied by translucent life-forms, ghosts of the past; their familiars at their feet.

In the fifth chair sat a young woman, aged twenty-five. She watched the proceedings with growing interest. This meeting could bring her news of the outside world, a world she should have been part of, a world she had heard so much about, but only seen in books.

All eyes turned towards Briony, who walked purposefully and directly towards Forrestiana, and respectfully gave her Primrose's scarf, the bracelet and clasp.

Every soul was now present.

Holding the bracelet up to the light, Forrestiana turned it slowly and reverently. Hundreds of aromatic candles shone their light onto the silver band and lit the brightest of diamonds, shaped like a rose. As it caught the candles' flickering flames, it sparkled brilliantly and sent shards of light in all directions around the Great Hall.

'I can remember when this was first crafted. I marvelled at its beauty then; I marvel at it still. Without your sacrifice on the night of the Great Flood, Sweet Briar, Villosa would never have survived,' Forrestiana remarked. 'This bracelet belongs to you. Please place it back on your wrist. It will help control the Dark Magic you possess. Then you can take the other band off,' she continued, indicating the plain silver bracelet on Briony's wrist. Forrestiana never called Sweet Briar, Briony; she hated the way people shortened names and words.

Briony took the treasured bracelet from Forrestiana's hands and slipped it back onto her wrist. She then took her place within the Circlet. She remembered the first time she had seen it; Jack had given it to her on her wedding day. However, she had no intention of removing the plain silver band either. Jack had made that too as soon as he realised his wedding gift had been lost. The bracelets had helped her control the Dark Magic she possessed.

Forrestiana sighed deeply, 'Let us hope your idea works, Sweet Briar. Hopefully, the bracelet that Jack now carries in his pocket and the scarf you made for Evelyn can help lure her from whatever place she has disappeared to. It would mean so much to have our family back together, but I feel it is a hopeless dream.'

Slowly and majestically, Forrestiana rose from her chair and walked gracefully to a round oak table situated in the middle of the Circlet. She placed Primrose's scarf on a velvet cushion, coloured in the deepest of reds, and then examined the silver clasp closely before placing it carefully in her pocket.

Forrestiana was a tall woman, her long hair was captured in a tight coil at the nape of her neck and her white dress trailed on the ground. It shimmered in the candlelight as she walked proudly back to her place within the Circlet. On her wrist, another diamond bracelet caught the flickering light of the many candles that illuminated the Circlet. Forrestiana oozed power.

Placing her hands in her lap, Forrestiana sat down, her back ramrod straight. She studied each member seated around the Circlet. Each member had their familiar sitting next to them. Her huge, brown bear, Bruin, sat next to her.

By her side sat her husband. There was no mistaking that Arvensis was still a tall, powerfully built man and as a ghost, he still had a formidable presence. He returned his wife's stare with a warm smile. For all of Arvensis' power he had the gentlest of natures. Arvensis adored his wife and his children. He would do anything for them. Felina, a wildcat, slept curled in a ball at his feet.

Sharna nestled comfortably on Briony's lap enjoying the fuss being lavished upon her. Briony, her eldest daughter, had a far-away look on her face. Forrestiana knew she was thinking of Jack.

Solis, their healer, had a kestrel perched on the edge of her chair. Solis was a gentle soul, and she sat patiently as Forrestiana looked at each of them. She had been instrumental in Briony's welfare since the night of her arrival. Solis had a big heart, a gentle voice and a kind nature. It made her a favourite to all in the Sanctum.

Umbro, the alchemist, was the oldest soul. He was not one to sit still. Umbro had his laboratory and his work and he was dedicated to both. At present, he was feeling slightly harassed, he knew he had to attend this meeting, but his mind was elsewhere. Umbro held the food bag that Reynard, the fox, had retrieved from a bin, the same bin that Elina had thrown it in earlier. He could not wait to examine the revolting, gooey mess in his laboratory. Umbro was deeply fascinated with its contents.

Umbro's familiar was a moth. Forrestiana knew it was with him, even though she could not see it.

The final member of the circle was Villosa, her dark raven-black hair was styled similarly to that of Forrestiana's. She wore a long, richly coloured pink gown and also bore a striking resemblance to Violette. Reynard, lay curled at her feet with his bushy tail curled over his nose. Villosa was the only living human in the Sanctum, and she was like a daughter to Forrestiana and Arvensis, who adored her. She was also the most colourful as all the souls wore white.

The meeting had been called to discuss the latest developments above ground. The kestrel, Sharna, Reynard and the moth had just returned from the Ancient Forest and had news that needed to be shared.

The moth had returned with news that Primrose was no longer hindered by a stone foot and had started to study her Ancient Tome. While the kestrel had also returned with the welcome news that she had succeeded in her task in bringing Primrose and Elina together. She also confirmed that they had both returned to the Ancient Tree and Elina had stayed.

'Tonight we need to discuss the increasing danger that threatens us,' Forrestiana began, 'the Darkness has greatly increased since Sweet Briar's death. It is beginning to affect many. My biggest fear,' she continued, 'is that Nastarana has some sort of plan to eliminate us once more. I would be grateful for any thoughts or suggestions that you may have.'

'We need to instigate contact with Primrose and Elina in order to search their minds,' Arvensis stated, 'We need to know for certain how powerful their magic is and which power is the most dominant. Then we need to find out how much control they have gained over their magic, especially where Primrose is concerned. It's a lot to ask, their power is new to them, but their help with Nastarana will be invaluable. They need to be warned about him too.'

'I agree. At the moment all signs are positive,' Forrestiana said, 'both girls are studying well and using their magic as the Tomes request. Primrose knows what will happen if she starts to use her magic for the worse. I also believe Dilly will be a good companion for her. Elina will also help curb her strong will.'

'How strong is Elina's magic?' Solis asked.

'No one knows; it is why I would like to examine her,' Forrestiana added. 'Both girls have the potential to become extremely powerful magicians, but I fear if they are not made aware of the danger that threatens us and them, there is a possibility they might do something extremely foolhardy, especially if they come across Nastarana or one of his drones. Those scarfs were a brilliant idea, Sweet Briar, at least they will receive a warning when something nearby is not to be trusted.'

'It was fortunate that Primrose inhaled some of Elina's magic for two reasons,' Umbro stated in his forthright manner. He placed the bag containing the remnants of the cake onto the floor, sighing audibly. He desperately wanted to carry out a detailed investigation on the substances it contained. He ran a hand through his thinning hair. It was something he was prone to do when agitated, 'Firstly, Elina's magic could have flared and that could have killed her. Secondly, Primrose absorbed so much of Elina's energy that it seems to have had a positive effect on her. Without knowing it, they seem to have done each other a massive favour.'

'Although Elina is showing an unusual ability to read people and animals correctly,' Arvensis added, 'her magic seems to have adapted. It will be interesting to see how that develops. It was a good idea, oh daughter mine, using your kestrel to orchestrate a meeting between the two girls.'

Villosa grew taller at her father's praise. Arvensis was in fact her grandfather, but Villosa considered him to be her father and she adored him.

Arvensis looked towards the round, oak table where Primrose's scarf nestled on its cushion. 'We also need to get that scarf to Primrose. She might need that for extra protection. It is a lovely piece of craftsmanship, Sweet Briar, unobtrusive as well. Are we to use a familiar to deliver it safely to her or teleportation, like Elina's Tome and bracelet?'

Briony stroked Sharna a little bit harder, avoiding her father's gaze. She had not told her parents about the letter she had sent along with the items.

'I believe Primrose will try and make contact again,' Forrestiana replied. 'She nearly achieved that on her first day in the Ancient Tree. She is also not a girl that easily lets things beat her. Her curiosity will get the better of her. I am sure she will come and soon, but if she does not, we will use Sharna again, and speaking of Sharna - I would like to send her to Violette's apartment again. I am glad that Elina decided to leave without needing a warning from her, but now it is important that we find out what side Violette is on. Umbro has made a device that will send us messages, once hidden inside the apartment.'

'What makes you suspicious of Violette?' Solis asked.

Forrestiana took out the silver clasp from her pocket and rolled it between her fingers, 'I know that she had something to do with this silver clasp that Sharna found at the base of the Ancient Tree, her mark is etched into the silver, but we have yet to discover how it got there. Violette still refuses to wear her bracelet. She has at times touched her scarf, but she needs to be physically touching both items for more than a few seconds for me to bring her here. Perhaps, we need to give her a scare. We could use Sharna for that task too. A strange choice for a familiar, what made you choose such a creature?' Forrestiana asked, turning towards Briony.

Briony lovingly stroked Sharna and smiled at the memory, but at the time she had been livid with Lettie, as everyone called Violette back then. 'In one of Violette's jealous rages she once called me a disgusting rat that should be confined to the sewers and shunned. I've always found rats to be intelligent creatures that most people go out of their way to avoid, so it seemed to me an excellent choice for a familiar.'

Arvensis laughed, amused at Briony's answer, 'It's a shame we can't teleport her here. I for one would like to ask her a question or two.'

'It is Primrose and Elina we need,' Forrestiana said, 'it is a shame you did not put instructions on how to use the bracelets in the letter you left for Elina, Sweet Briar. Do not think, I am not aware that you used Sharna to heal Jack's leg as well.'

Briony looked down at her hands in her lap, her translucent curls hiding her face. She should have known her mother knew about the letter. She had expected a bigger reaction from her; Briony realised she had gotten off rather lightly. However, the mention of Jack's name caused her eyes to water. She missed Jack and the wolves. She knew he had been struggling with his leg and could not help give her familiar an extra task to do - to heal his leg. She also knew it was forbidden.

'Using the rat was a clever idea, Sweet Briar,' Forrestiana continued, 'do not think that anything goes unnoticed here, but in future, anytime a familiar is sent to the other world, it is imperative that its task is discussed first... and it does not stray from it. There could have been consequences; everyone is being watched carefully above ground. This time we were lucky, so was Jack.'

Briony looked up and met Forrestiana's eyes; her mother's eyes were full of amusement and love. Briony had wondered as a child at how easily her mother could read her thoughts, now she knew it was all down to magic.

'So, it's decided then,' Arvensis concluded, 'Sharna will visit Violette and place a transmitter in her apartment, and a message will be delivered to the Ancient Tree regarding the bracelets.'

'I would rather the girls made their own way here,' Forrestiana added, bringing the meeting to a close, 'If one of our familiars were caught with that kind of message the consequences would be unthinkable. We will wait a few more days and see what happens. I cannot have all of our good work jeopardised.'

Forrestiana stood up, looked towards Arvensis and held out her hand. Arvensis took it and placed it on his heart before standing next to her. Both looked at their daughters and smiled lovingly, before leaving the Circlet.

Briony hastily picked up Sharna and returned to her room. She needed to see if Sharna had been successful in using her magic to heal Jack's leg and she had just the mirror to do it. She couldn't wait to see his face once more and hopefully send him a message too. She would then sleep.

She had not realised how exhausted she had become in her other world. Maintaining a protective barrier around the Ancient Tree had drained much of her magic. In her heart, she was certain that the Tree was going to play a crucial part in safeguarding their future. The feeling had proved correct; it now sheltered both of her daughters.

Briony's thoughts returned to Primrose and the stone statue. It had suffered badly from her neglect. At first, the loss of her memory had stopped her from remembering how to cast the more complicated spells correctly and using the Dark Magic had scared her dreadfully, since she had forgotten how to dispose of it safely. She had feared the Darkness would eventually gain control over her, but with Jack's help and encouragement she had learnt to use it sparingly, but not soon enough to master Primrose's 'Changings'. The statue had begun to crumble bit by bit and as each piece fell Briony's guilt had grown.

It was not until that awful day, when her eyes had locked onto the golden dust swirling around the brambles, and she had heard the struggles of Primrose trying to free herself, that another hazy memory began to return. She remembered she had had a child in her arms on the night of the Great Flood, and she had struggled hard to save it, but something had gotten in her way. The returning memory had hit her like a sledgehammer. Briony had begun to believe she had made a colossal mistake. She feared she had turned her own daughter to stone. The child she had held in her arms on the night of the Great Flood had a fuzz of dark hair, but her child had had a halo of golden curls, just like Primrose! The realisation of the truth had broken her heart!

Tonight, at the meeting, Briony had looked at the gooey mess that Reynard had brought back with him and received another shock. She realised that Violette must have used some kind of disguising spell on both herself and Jack. Briony believed the spell must have been in the tonics or the cakes that Violette had sent them regularly. It was the only explanation she could think of that had prevented her from recognising Primrose as her own child.

As Forrestiana and Arvensis returned to their room, Forrestiana remembered a time when all thirteen ornately carved chairs had been occupied by living relatives and friends. Now thanks to Jack following the burial ritual correctly the soul of Sweet Briar had been returned to them.

Unfortunately, Jack believed that if he completed the list, his wife would return to him, but she knew it would take more than that for that wish to come true. She smiled slightly at the extra items her daughter had added to the list in order to keep her husband busy after her death. However, if he did manage to complete the tasks, she and Arvensis would be in his debt forever.

Forrestiana's thoughts drifted to the chairs around the Circlet. Five souls and one young girl now occupied these seats. Each one of these souls could now watch and influence like-minded beings above ground by using their familiars or the old magic that radiated from the Ancient Tree, but it was the other empty seven seats that gave her cause for concern.

New names had been carved on two of them now, replacing the magicians that had died in the first conflict with Nastarana.

Another member refused all contact with them. She had cut off all ties and would give no reason why. They weren't even sure if Violette could be trusted anymore.

Two had been lost for many years; no news or clues had been discovered or received of their fate since the night of the Great Flood. Their souls were considered to be extinguished and lost to them forever. Forrestiana tried hard to remember the faces of her son, Darius and her daughter, Evelyn. It was a shame that Sweet Briar had lost her memory in the Great Flood. Now, hopefully, her memories would be fully restored and some clues might finally be discovered that could help solve the mystery of their missing son and youngest daughter.

Another magician had relinquished his magic as a result of a war fought against the Darkness many years ago, on the condition that the lives of herself, Arvensis, Umbro and his daughter, Solis were spared. Jack Hugonis had made a huge sacrifice on their behalf. Forrestiana believed that Jack was also under some sort of spell cast by Nastarana or Violette or both. She could not understand why he seemed to be oblivious to Nastarana's rising power, and his not recognising Primrose as his own daughter had been unbelievable.

Two future members had at present no clue that they had a position within the Circlet, but Forrestiana had faith that that was about to change. Surely, either Primrose or Elina would find a way to contact them.

The last former member would never be allowed to enter the Sanctum again, while she still lived. This magician, who believed he was the greatest this world had ever seen, had caused too much pain and suffering. Nastarana would never be allowed back in their Sanctum. Forrestiana felt his power increasing every day. She knew for certain he was planning another attack, his third, but this time she would be ready. This time they would win.

Arvensis squeezed his wife's hand in comfort, aware of both her sadness and the hope that burned fiercely in her heart. Forrestiana desperately wanted her family to be reunited and the battle against the Darkness won. That hope burned fiercely in his heart as well.

16. MASTERING MAGIC

Primrose and Elina followed a strict routine that involved study, practise and further practise outside in the forest. What was read during the morning was practised that afternoon and revisited until each lesson was mastered. Their mother's letters had created lots of unanswered questions: Where was she? Where had the Tomes, bracelets and letters come from? What was the danger she had wrote about? Why had their mother's magic not kept her young like Violette? What or who controlled the magic in the Tree? Why did Violette act in such a way? Was Violette the Darkness or was it something else?

They knew that their father would be able to answer some of their questions, but looking for him in the forest would take up precious time, especially, when they knew where he would be on the night of the Full Moon. So, for now the girls practised and practised hard, believing that their lives could depend on it. They were determined not to be caught out by the danger they felt was looming or by what their mother had hinted at in her letters.

The time had finally come for Primrose to practise using her Dark Magic inside the Ancient Tree. She waited until she was on her own. She felt Elina would disapprove and believe she was not ready, but Primrose was determined to master both types of magic and in her mind the sooner the better. Even so, she was nervous. She had not tried using it since receiving the scare on her first full day in the Ancient Tree. She had not forgotten the strong desire to touch the panel, and the blast of energy that had shot across the room or the way the Dark Magic beckoned.

Cautiously, she removed her silver bracelet and flexed the fingers on her left hand and took a deep breath. At first, she concentrated on producing the smallest amount of Dark Magic; a thin trail of what appeared to be black smoke materialised almost immediately.

The next step should have been simple, if it had not been for the sudden, loud noise Shadow made as he upturned his water bowl. Primrose only lost concentration for a split second as she spun round to see what the commotion was, but this was enough to allow the magic to flow unheeded.

Instead of reabsorbing the magic back into her hand as she had intended, she accidently breathed some of the dust in. Without a shield to protect her mind, her resulting headache was the worst she had ever experienced. Not only was the pain so bad, but she also felt the return of her vicious side and the need to hurt something or someone, and then she felt nothing, absolutely nothing. Primrose had collapsed!

Shadow ran upstairs to Elina's room as fast as he could, seeking help. Dilly, meanwhile, watched Primrose twitch, convulse and then stop moving altogether. Dilly tried nuzzling, licking and pushing Primrose with her snout, but nothing. Primrose lay still and unresponsive.

Elina entered the room quickly and knelt beside Primrose and tried to locate a pulse - it was weak and erratic, but it was there! Shadow whimpered. He felt he was nothing but trouble, he always seemed to cause some kind of mishap, but then he remembered a voice from the past - 'you don't tell anyone about this or what I'm about to do. If you do, I can cook a mean wolf cub pie.'

Shadow nudged Elina's hands, 'Put one of your hands on her heart and the other on her forehead, that's what she did to you.'

Using his snout, Shadow made sure that Elina's hands were in the exact same spots that he had seen Violette do, so many nights ago.

'Then she chanted something,' Shadow continued, trying hard to remember the words that Violette had muttered that night.

'Who said something, Shadow?' Elina asked gently, realising Shadow was trying extremely hard to remember something important.

'Violette, when she brought you round, it was something like... I can't remember and then she clapped and you and Dilly got better,' he replied, annoyed with himself, because he could not remember the words, but they had sounded so strange to him at the time.

'It must have been a healing spell; there must be one in her book,' Elina rose to her feet and went to the table on which Primrose's Tome lay. It was opened on the page instructing her on the use of Dark Magic. Elina sighed and wondered why Primrose couldn't have waited for her. As she scanned the open page, the book started to vibrate. Pages were turned back quickly to reveal a reversing spell in the form of a chant; Elina had not done a thing!

Elina took hold of the tome with shaking hands and placed it on the floor next to Primrose and nervously began the chant:

Out of the dark, into the light
Fight the magic, with all your might.
Out of the dark, come back to me
Fight the evil, forever be!

When the chant was finished, she clapped her hands just as Shadow had told her earlier.

Primrose began to stir slightly, unsure of what had happened to her. She looked around and was greeted by a sea of angry eyes. It took a full hour for her to recover completely. Luckily, the only sign of her first experiment with Dark Magic was a massive throbbing headache and a dreadful feeling of guilt. Dilly was not at all happy with her.

'This Dark Magic malarkey really freaks me out. It makes me horribly nervous,' Primrose admitted, slipping her bracelet back on. 'I suppose I'm going to have to try that one again!'

'Agreed, but wait until I'm with you next time!' Elina scolded, 'Just because you're inside the Ancient Tree, doesn't mean you should forget your protection spells. You gave us all a horrible fright.'

Primrose gave a sheepish look of apology to Elina, Dilly and Shadow, but she knew she would have to do a lot more before Dilly would forgive her.

Meanwhile, Shadow lay with his nose on his paws with his ears flopped forward, wondering if Violette would actually turn him into a mean wolf pie. He had promised never to tell anyone of what he saw that night when Violette had healed Elina, Dilly and himself. Everyone had thought Elina's magic had cured them all. He knew neither Elina nor Primrose would allow that to happen, but it still worried him slightly. His eyes followed Elina as she walked towards him and said:

'How about we put Vile Vi in a pie instead?'

'Only if you want the biggest bout of indigestion ever,' Primrose laughed, 'I'll never let her hurt you, Shadow. Thank you for saving me tonight. You did well. And you definitely deserve another giant, juicy piece of steak.'

Shadow wagged his tail, salivating nicely over the floor, his troubles nearly forgotten.

The next day, as the sun was shining warmly in a forest opening, Primrose decided it was time to practise a particular spell involving the creation of magical energy spheres or orbs. They would then be controlled by either hand or arm signals and if possible their minds. It was the start of using their thoughts to transfer energy to move objects or magical rays. Primrose was extremely excited at the idea and finally felt her magic was getting somewhere. Today would be the day that she would use both types of magic; it both thrilled and scared her.

Elina, on the other hand, was hoping to use her mind to either energise the spheres or try to take them from her sister.

Remaining hidden and alone inside her protective barrier, Primrose cupped her hands in front of her. Gently, she began to rotate her hands in opposite directions, concentrating on her right hand until golden dust formed. She then shaped it into a golden sphere and let her hands drop down to her sides - the sphere hovered in front of her at waist height.

Concentrating hard, Primrose moved her hands upwards and forwards, the sphere moved away from her and started to soar as it followed the directions dictated by her hands. As her confidence grew, Primrose formed several more orbs and made them dance.

Elina, wearing the yellow cloak, stood outside the barrier and made sure Primrose and the orbs remained undetected. When she felt sure that Primrose could maintain the barrier and manoeuvre the spheres consistently, she entered the barrier.

Primrose smiled at Elina as she entered the barrier and repeated the spell for her, enjoying the sight of several orbs gliding through the air. Suddenly, Primrose clapped her hands and the spheres popped gently and golden dust sprinkled softly to the ground. The grass grew greener and stood taller as the glittering dust settled and coated the ground like dew, slowly the pinprick dots of light extinguished, disappearing completely.

'Wow!' Primrose said, 'Time to do that again. This time, Lina, try to see if you can take some away from me. If I create magic, I need to know if I can keep it. I would not like anyone to use it against me.'

Once more Primrose created golden orbs. At first, Elina concentrated on just one orb and managed to gain control of it. Primrose clapped; every orb, bar the one captured by Elina, popped gently as before. Elina followed Primrose's example and clapped. Golden dust showered both of the young wolves, who had just entered the barrier after one of their adventures away from the girls. Excited by the flickering dust, they chased the floating specks and tried to eat them before they fell to the ground.

'We might have to be a little bit more careful where the dust settles, Lina. We don't want to have giant wolves on our hands,' Primrose stated.

'I'd rather have giant wolves in our hands than someone else's,' Elina added seriously, looking at both Dilly and Shadow; they seemed to be growing very quickly. She wondered briefly if that was to do with their magic or the amount of food that both wolves managed to tuck away each day.

Primrose continued to practise making and controlling different sized orbs and soon learnt to manipulate them expertly, she tried to be one step ahead of Elina to avoid their capture. Both girls were extremely competitive and were enjoying themselves immensely.

Primrose's hands and arms moved gracefully, tracing patterns in the air; the orbs mirrored every turn. It was a huge improvement to the awkward movements Primrose had used earlier that afternoon. Elina pretended to use her arms and hands and copied many of her sister's movements, but secretly she probed Primrose's mind and eventually forestalled all her movements and captured every sphere.

Elina, also had to put into practise the lessons she had studied.

Primrose tried her best, but was unable to recapture a single sphere. She watched Elina intently and suddenly, frustrated beyond belief, clapped her hands against her head and declared, 'I give up! I can't recapture them. Your arm movements make no sense to me. Where am I going wrong? Give me a clue!'

'But, Primmy, if I give you a clue, how on earth are you going to figure out where you're going wrong? I could be an ugly sister, bending you to my will and… I haven't heard that special word,' Elina laughed.

'Bending you to my will?' Primrose narrowed her eyes, as she repeated a phrase Elina had said, 'You were reading my mind, of all the sneaky, underhand…'

'Now, now,' Elina teased, 'lesson learnt. Remember, not everyone is going to be on our side and play nice. You need to keep your shield secure at all times.'

Primrose laughed. 'Dilly is a great assistant, but you are priceless. By the way, where are the wolves?' Primrose asked suddenly, 'I've been too engrossed to notice where they went, that's another lesson I need to learn or people around me could get hurt.'

'They got bored with the orbs and went off to explore. They're on their way back as we speak.'

Elina held out her hands to the sky and the orbs landed gently into her palms. She gathered them together to form one orb and then gently squeezed her hands together, the orb disappeared. Primrose looked on amazed.

'How did you know that would happen?'

'I didn't,' Elina replied equally baffled, 'I sensed it. Do you think I might have some of your magic in me now? After all they were your orbs.'

'Can't imagine why you think I have the answer to that one, mind you, Lina, time will tell. Do you want some of the black orbs as well?' she laughed. 'Because, believe it or not, they're the ones I need to practise with now.' Slowly Primrose dried her nervous hands on her skirt.

Primrose repeated the procedure, as before, but this time she concentrated on her left hand and created the smallest of black orbs by compressing the black dust. She then sent it away and practised manoeuvring the orb quickly and slowly, turning its course both sharply and smoothly. Once she was sure she could control it just as well as the golden orbs, she looked at Elina - a warning, to let her know she was about to clap her hands.

Primrose was more than a bit disappointed with the small pop emitted from the tiny orb as it disintegrated, she thought Dark Magic was supposed to be scary. Still looking at the small particles floating harmlessly in the air, she stood up straight, placed her hands on her hips and muttered something indistinguishable under her breath. She turned towards Elina, 'Well, that was a total flop, a waste of energy and time, I should have been braver and made a larger…'

A sudden, large vibration surged through the air; hundreds of flaming sparks shot out in all directions. Dilly and Shadow, who had just returned to the glade were showered with burning embers; both ran as fast as they could, tails between their legs, as more burning embers followed them.

Primrose, spinning around quickly saw further sparks coming straight at her. She stood still totally transfixed by the burning embers; all she could think of was - how on earth could something so small create so much energy?

Elina acted quickly, she imagined a shield around the pair of them and sent another mental shield towards the fleeing wolves. She then stood up straight, criss-crossed her hands above her head, and brought her arms down quickly in an arc to her sides, fluttering her fingers at the same time to create a short, sharp, heavy bout of rain - extinguishing every spark.

'Underestimated that a bit, definitely need to master that

one,' Primrose said rather sheepishly, looking apologetically at Elina.

'And make it up to the wolves; that might not be so easy.'

Dilly and Shadow had returned to the practise arena, and two pairs of angry, accusing eyes bored into Primrose.

'Steak tonight, for the pair of you,' Primrose offered in way of an apology.

Dilly was unimpressed, Shadow on the other hand loved steak and was ready to forgive Primrose anything in return for food.

'And you, Dilly, can share my bed tonight. Lina, I think we will leave the other sphere combinations for another day or at least until I've mastered this one. Tomorrow, I will repeat this spell, but I would like you on the outside of the barrier, just to make sure it holds out under that amount of energy, can't be too careful! That was a really cool idea to use the rain and a shield. You know, we are going to make one awesome team. Thank you for getting me out of trouble.'

'That's what sisters are for,' Elina replied, 'that was quite a show from one small piece of Dark Magic, don't think I will be squeezing any of them; you can keep those ones.'

As they walked back to the Tree, Primrose said, 'There's something else I want to try tonight, and I need the safety of the Tree for that. After reading mother's letter, on my first night inside the Tree, I was sitting in the rocking chair and something strange happened to me. It scared me quite a bit, but I'm ready to try it out again. It will be good having you there with me. You always seem to know what to do when something goes wrong and that gives me confidence.'

'Are you going to tell me what you intend to do?' Elina asked after Primrose went quiet for a time.

'A long-distance telephone call,' Primrose answered mysteriously. 'I'll explain after we've had something to eat.'

After eating another delicious meal, Elina tried to relax but an odd feeling kept coming over her. Her eyes darted from the cradle to a panel, and then back again. The hairs on the back of her neck stood up on end and a cold shiver ran up her back. She felt uneasy, not in a dreadful way, but as though her mind was trying to get to grips with a message but could not quite grasp its meaning. Elina blamed it on the last chapter she had been reading concerning meditation.

Elina closed her eyes and tried once more to clear her mind. She needed to feel relaxed before helping Primrose practise her new spell, but the strange feeling persisted. Sighing deeply, she stood up and walked across to the cradle.

'Are you alright, Lina?' Primrose enquired, noticing how restless her sister had become.

'Not sure, but something's bothering me.' Elina stroked the wooden, top rail of the cradle, looked around, stepped in front of it, then crossed the room to the panel and studied the black centre and the unusual markings. She then looked at the trap door and the cold feeling down her back intensified.

'Do you know how those markings were made?' Elina asked, looking at the panel again.

'No, but I think it was from a blast of Dark Magic, probably one of our ancestors practising with one of those black spheres,' Primrose suggested, 'I felt something myself as I looked at that panel, possibly some kind of residual energy.'

'I don't think so,' Elina added, preoccupied once more with the markings.

'I wouldn't touch that if I were you,' Primrose warned, raising her voice, 'My left hand really wanted to, and it took a lot of control on my part to keep it by my side. I need to know a bit more about my dark side before I touch that thing again. Elina, don't you dare!' she screamed.

Elina placed both hands on the panel; then rested her head between them. She listened intently and sensed a connection. Tracing the strange markings with her fingers, she followed them until they touched its blackened centre. That is when she sensed it. Dawn, Dawn had been here, and something else too - a weakened life form. She sensed desperation, despair and utter loneliness.

'We have a lodger,' Elina spoke at last, 'Whatever happened here started at this spot,' she said as she walked towards the table, 'It surged powerfully and smashed into a door, I think this panel was once a door,' Elina paled, she felt sick and faint. 'Our mother was entering that trap door when the blast hit her too.'

Primrose rushed over and caught Elina as she fell, 'It took her into the flood waters, Primmy. It swept her away with another.'

Shadow and Dilly, who had been watching Elina's strange behaviour started to whimper anxiously. They saw her fall and rushed over to help and comfort her. For one awful moment they thought Elina had once again had her magic drained from her and was slipping away from them; memories of that awful day flooded back.

When Elina felt better, Primrose took her up to her bathroom and showed her the carving above her bath. Two women, each with a child, were watched by a man, and another girl played in the river with another man. In the top right corner two faces looked down on the family from the heavens and in the top left corner an indistinguishable, unsettling figure looked on too.

'I believe the carving shows Briony, our mother, and her family. I believe the figures in the sky to be our ancestors looking over us. I think I am one of those babies,' Primrose said quietly.

'I think you're right, but I feel nothing but worn out. I'm tired after that last vision,' Elina said.

'You're not going to like this very much, Lina, but I believe I can get in touch with them. In the letter it says I will meet our mother in an unexpected way. We need their help. If we have a lodger…' Primrose paused, 'In fact, I'm certain we have a lodger. There's part of the Ancient Tree that has no leaves, in the same part I've seen a hole at the top of the Tree and at times a wisp of something coming from it, like smoke. I think it's Dark Magic. So, I would like to try and open up a line of communication tonight. I think I nearly opened it once before, but I panicked and the feeling stopped. What do you think?'

'I think you intended to try this tonight even without my say-so,' Elina smiled at her, 'If you want to go ahead with it, let's hope the line you open is the couple in the sky and not that thing,' she added with some concern, looking at the other corner of the carving.

'Nice one Lina, as though I don't feel nervous enough already!'

17. THE SUMMONER

Darius, or the Summoner, as Dawn used to called him, sank to his knees and pulled the cloak tightly around his emaciated form. He was desperate and knew he would soon have to give into the Darkness and the voice that bombarded his mind at every opportunity. The continuous struggle between the Darkness and Light was almost over; he felt he would soon be lost within its folds for ever. His magic that had initially kept the evil at bay had almost gone; just a small thread of Gold Magic was keeping him on the edge of sanity.

Once he had been a good man, sometimes a bit wild and thoughtless, but on the whole a good soul. His entrapment had caught him totally unawares. The full extent of his wife's unhappiness had finally got the better of her that night long, long ago. He had been a fool - a stupid, ignorant fool. Besotted by his wife, he had not seen her betrayal coming. He wondered, sadly, whether she had ever loved him.

He remembered the shock, amazement and horror, when his wife had forcefully aimed a blast of magic directly at him; it knocked him violently and painfully backwards and into a small storage cupboard. The air had been totally knocked out of him as he had staggered and fell helplessly, hitting his head against a protruding shelf. She had closed the door and left him, crumpled in a ball, bleeding and unconscious.

'Now, she lives in a beautiful apartment and has everything money could buy. She has such a perfect life. All this could be yours. Just let go, trust me,' the voice taunted him.

Darius stroked his chest, which still bore the horrific scars of that magical burn, a permanent reminder of his wife's betrayal and of his ignorance.

'Remember, revenge is sweet,' the voice of Darkness invaded his mind, tempting him to give him.

When he had woken from that magical blast, he had found that he shared his prison with a beautiful, tawny owl. He smiled slightly as he remembered the look it had given him. The owl had swivelled its head from side to side and studied him just as intently. It surprised him to see that it was tethered to a perch by a silver chain, and positioned beside the smallest of openings to the outside world. The opening was to become his only glimpse of the world, the world he had once roamed at will and took for granted.

'And you still can, just like your wife. Roam to your heart's content. Just let go. Trust me.'

He had tried using his Gold Magic to free himself, but to no avail. He was locked inside with powerful magic, much stronger than his own.

Now, every minute of every day was an exhausting struggle: the voice that kept invading his mind and spirits picked at him constantly; wearing him down. Trapped inside a ridiculously small storage cupboard for countless, endless years had eventually taken its toll and turned him into the pitiful creature he now was.

Even his desperate cries for help had never been heard. With his magic almost depleted and his spirit at its lowest ebb, he was so, so tempted to just let go. If he let the Darkness have him, his struggles would be over. But an inner voice urged him on and told him never give up, the voice of his sister, Briony. The memory warmed him. Deep down he knew the promises of his tempter were false.

'Untrue, untrue - freedom and power is just a thought away.'

Only a short while ago, he had hoped, almost believed, that his incarceration would soon end. After many years of inactivity, someone had triggered the motion sensor and entered the Ancient Tree, and Primrose's home computer had turned on. He thought warmly of his old gaming partner. He had hoped to train her through the game so that she could protect herself from the Darkness and eventually free him. He knew Primrose, his sister's child, would eventually possess magic, but for some unknown reason the computer connection had been lost and so had his chance for freedom.

The spark of hope lit that night had grown into an enormous fire - the knowledge that freedom could at last be his. He had grabbed the chance eagerly with both hands, but for nothing. The flame had been extinguished just as quickly, and his world had come crashing down. The connection had been lost and his calls for help went unnoticed. He wondered if someone had really entered the Ancient Tree or whether his mind was playing tricks on him.

In his eagerness for freedom he had dropped his guard and lost his only companion. A sense of guilt washed over him at that memory.

'But you can be free. I can make all of your dreams come true. I never let anyone down.'

Darius tried desperately to ignore the voice. He tried hard to keep positive, but sometimes that voice seemed to know how to penetrate his mind and then it became more forceful, more persistent, more persuasive. He told himself to fill his mind with memories and try to block it out. He wanted to keep what little magic he had left. He hoped and prayed something might still happen; he would need his magic then.

At first, he had struck up a friendship with the owl. He used his magic to feed and clean them both and the bird had become his eyes and ears to the world outside. It had kept him abreast of everything that happened around the forest. But as the years progressed, he became lonelier and succumbed to the dangers of isolation. His temper frayed and he freely admitted that he had become an extremely unpredictable task master, especially when the effects of the Dark Magic began to affect him.

In fact, at that moment, he was extremely embarrassed by just how brutal and cruel he had become; that poor, enslaved bird had endured countless beatings from him. He did not blame it one bit for not coming back to him; he would have done the same, if their places had been reversed. He knew this feeling of regret would cease, all he had to do was give in to the Darkness.

'That's right, give in. No more feelings of guilt. No more loneliness. No more soul searching. Everything you could ever wish for will be yours. Trust me!'

Trapped in this ridiculously small room, he had not slept properly for years - there was no room to lie down properly. He could not exercise either as space was limited. As for a bath, he yearned to soak his wasted body and become clean again, yet another unfulfilled dream. He glanced round at the black, encrusted walls with despair. He knew his skin was also thickly embedded with the toxic particles too.

'But it doesn't have to be. Let go, come to me.'

Magic had trapped him here and his magic had worsened his imprisonment. There was no way out unless he chose the darkest of routes.

'Well done, choose me, trust me.'

Once, Darius had possessed both types of magic and when the Dark Magic surged, he had to use his Gold Magic to disperse it, but it was a dangerous method to use, especially as the dust was as trapped as he was; there was nowhere for it to go. The inside of the cupboard was now coated in a thick layer of accumulated black dust. This not only made the space smaller, but sealed him inside as brilliantly as the Gold Magic on the other side kept him out of the main rooms of the Ancient Tree. The black dust was lethal when breathed in; it could turn you mad, crazy or violent.

After many years, Darius thought he could qualify on all accounts. Mad, because he could hear voices and wanted to talk back. Crazy, because he had loved a woman, who had not loved him in return, and violent because of the disgusting way he had treated the owl and the feelings of rage that at times consumed him.

For a moment, he wondered if it was his wife that had entered the Ancient Tree, if that was the case, he stood no chance of freedom.

'But this need not be; you can be free in a matter of seconds. Trust me.'

Violette, or Lettie as he loved to call her, had betrayed him; she had given him a fake, duplicate belt that night. Unfortunately, he had only discovered this after his incarceration. The belt had been crafted by a great magician called Hugonis. The leather was etched, depicting his favourite forest scenes and fastened with a silver clasp, shaped like a wolf's head; the wolf's eyes were pure diamonds. Hugonis had also made bracelets for his sisters and mother, as well as special gauntlets for his father to help him control the Dark Magic he possessed.

Lettie must have switched the belts that night without his knowledge. He hoped the real belt still hung somewhere inside the Ancient Tree, if only he could get out of this room and find it. If he had that belt now and not the fake one that hung loosely around his waist, he would have been able to escape. The belt would have allowed him to teleport himself to a safe place. Lettie knew of the belt's powers. Lettie had betrayed him in more ways than he could count. A wave of pure frustration and anger washed over him.

'So, let's show her the error of her ways.'

Recently, he had become extremely excited; the owl had brought him exciting news. It had mentioned names he had recognised. Jack, his friend, was looking for Primrose and his sister Evelyn. Hope grew, but then his mind became confused when the bird mentioned Briony had just died. He thought she had died on the same night he was imprisoned, swept away in that huge wave.

In fact, he had thought all his family was dead; his parents at the hands of his uncle in a battle fought long ago and his sisters on the night of the flood. If only he had known this earlier, if only the bird would come back.

He really needed the owl, he could give it messages to take to Jack, but every time he summoned it, the bird refused to come. He feared the owl had been killed too. Now, he had no clue what to do next.

What was it that Briony, his sister, told him to say whenever he struggled? That's it; it was never to give up. Stay positive.

'No, no, she always told you to take the easy way and give up!'

'No! Never!' he shouted loudly and suddenly realised his error. He should not have called out. The voice became more persistent when he called out, and he did not have a lot of magic left to keep it at bay. He was forced to use it and fast. He snapped his fingers and the voice was gone, and regretfully, another piece of precious Gold Magic was gone forever.

Good deeds had to be done to maintain Gold Magic and that was impossible in this pathetic, stupid, irritating, claustrophobic, dirty, little room! His temper flared and boiled within him. Darius was in danger as he struggled and fought to keep himself sane. He was finding it so, so difficult and he was so, so tired. He pulled his filthy, black coat, round his wafer, thin body and hugged himself tightly and prayed for one last time.

18. PRIMROSE TRIES SOMETHING NEW

Elina watched Primrose intently, probing her mind for any signs of anxiety or fear. Primrose sat in the rocking chair, hands on the arm rests and eyes closed. She concentrated her mind on the carving and the image of the two friendly faces that gazed down on the family group.

After a while Primrose seemed to shimmer, but no lines of worry marked her countenance. Elina noticed that her face had changed slightly, probably from all the fresh air giving it a healthier tone; her hair too seemed to have developed a tinge of auburn. She thought it was strange that she had not noticed it before, but then Primrose would probably have had something to say if she was caught staring at her for any length of time.

Her eyes flickered to the diary, Primrose had been insistent that she read some of the passages. Although Elina still felt as though she was prying, it also gave her something to do while her sister tried to open a 'line of communication'. Flicking through the diary, Elina let it fall open on a page near the beginning and began to read the following entry:-

Dear Diary

Had such a great day today, mother had to go out somewhere, got dropped off at Briony's. What a result!!!

You'll never guess what Auntie Briony let me do - stroke a wolf! I actually stroked a wolf!!!! And it wasn't a little one, it was huge and she was called Luna. When I grow up I'm going to have my own wolf.

We also picked zillions of berries. Briony taught me all the names. She also said that if I keep scoffing them we won't have enough to make a pudding and a cake!!!! Yummy! I got really, really, really messy too.

Auntie said my cake was the bestest she'd ever seen and I should take it home to show mother. I wanted to share it with her instead.

I hate, hate, hate, hate her!!!!!!!!!!!!!

She is the vilest mother on planet earth! My cake is ugly! I am a useless cook! I'm not to bring anymore cooking home! I wish, wish, wish I could stay with Auntie Briony. My mother is the vilest Vi ever to live.

Raising her head from the diary, Elina stared at Primrose; she remembered baking cakes with her mother too. She knew that her mother would have eaten the cake and told Primrose it was the best she had ever tasted, even if she had used salt instead of sugar.

It was a shame that her mother had not been aware that Primrose had actually been her daughter. She wondered, once more, why Violette had pretended that Primrose was hers, when she obviously had no motherly instincts. As she gazed at Primrose again, she noticed that the trance like state had deepened and that she was still totally relaxed. Elina turned a few more pages over and started to read another entry.

Primrose and Elina were not to know, but that cake was a favourite of Briony's. It was also a cake that only Briony knew how to make. Violette could not have anything in her home that showed Briony was getting her memory back. That would have put Briony's life in danger.

Sunday, August 16th

Dear Diary,

Mother slapped me today, not just once! It hurt. But I wouldn't cry. She said it was my fault. I found her make-up and I wanted to look grown up and just as pretty as she is. Instead she laughed at me and told me I looked like some kind of messy monster. I'm glad I ruined her make-up - it was the lovely expensive stuff! I'm glad I made her mad too. I detest her. It's going to take years to pay for the new lot. I wish someone else was my mum. Auntie would have let me and I bet she would have let me make her up too!

Her heart went out to Primrose, that was exactly what her mother would have done. Not only that, but she would have shown her how to apply it as well, even though her mother rarely used make-up.

Violette, on the other hand, had come home that night and received the biggest shock of her life. Primrose with make-up on bore a strong resemblance to Briony and Violette had panicked big time. Nastarana was due to visit at any second and if he saw Primrose and the resemblance to Briony, they would both be in dreadful trouble. Primrose had been sent to her room and the door locked!

In fact, after that day, Violette had made a habit of making Primrose disappear every time Nastarana was due. It was far safer that way!

Elina heard Primrose mutter something, but it was too indistinct to make out what it was; she placed the diary into her lap. Primrose was definitely speaking.

'Is my mother here?' she heard Primrose demand.

There was a pause and Primrose began to speak again, 'How do I know you speak the truth?'

Primrose's voice held a note of defiance, but Elina still sensed no signs of worry or fear. It was obvious she was having some kind of conversation and had successfully opened the line of communication with their ancestors.

'We believe the Ancient Tree has a lodger. Elina is convinced that whatever it is means us no harm, but it is close to death.'

Elina was momentarily startled when she heard her name mentioned, but she was also sure that she had heard the words 'Ancient Tree' somewhere before and recently. Primrose had always referred to the tree as home or just called it the Tree when speaking to her. She had been unaware that the tree had a name and had never thought to ask! Now she wondered where she had heard or seen the name before.

Primrose's shimmering form started to pulsate quickly, a sign of excitement and not fear.

'Lina,' Primrose called, 'if I disappear for a while, don't be alarmed. I am safe, very safe. I will be back.'

To the astonishment of Elina, and more importantly Dilly, Primrose vanished into thin air! Dilly went mad, she ran to the chair, sniffed, whimpered and commenced a frantic and thorough search of the floor and the air - her desperate sniffs resembled a powerful hoover.

Shadow opened one eye; after living with Violette for a while, he was used to strange happenings and watched his sister's search with a calm air of detachment. He knew she was wasting her time, he had seen Violette disappear sometimes; especially when she thought he was out on one of his forays.

'Dilly, come, come here,' Elina called to the wolf, wanting to calm her down.

Reluctantly, Dilly came to Elina's side, 'Primrose is fine, Dilly. She has gone to see Briony. She'll be back soon. I promise.'

Dilly began to settle, comforted by both Elina's voice and the touch of her gentle fingers as they massaged the space between her ears. Finally, Dilly understood - if Elina was not alarmed, then why should she be? However, Elina was hoping that it would not be one promise that she might have to break.

While Elina waited for Primrose's return, she turned her attention once more to the diary. This time she turned to the end of the book and read the last two entries.

Monday, March 11th

Dear Diary,

Best day ever. Top of the year, I rock!!!! I am the best! I even beat Stella the Speller. She's been top of the class for 3 whole years and she wasn't happy when she came 2nd. Couldn't wait to tell Vile Vi. Should have known better, think I would have learnt by now, but no, I go and open my big, fat mouth! She just sat there, in front of the stupid mirror and painted her stupid, old nails one by one. Didn't look at me once! That annoyed me big time. She didn't even pretend to listen to me.

Got my own back, annoyed her so much she took me to Briony's and Briony made me a special cake for being top of the class and the year. I love Briony. Wish she was my mother. I asked if I could stay some nights at the cottage. Auntie said she would ask my mum.

Tuesday, March 12th

Dear Diary,

Why? Why? Why? She's done it again! Ruined my life! I can never, ever stay over at Briony's, and if I keep on, she will never ever let me visit her again. Briony has let me down too!!! She has agreed with my mum and won't tell me why!!! It's so not fair. Nothing's fair. Well if they want trouble, I'll give them trouble with a great big T.

All of a sudden, it seemed so much clearer to Elina why Primrose was so angry with her mother. Primrose had felt rejected, abandoned and unloved by her, especially as her mother was someone that she had clearly adored, and maybe, the only person who had treated her kindly.

Elina had no need to read any more. Placing the diary back on the table, she suddenly remembered where she had seen the words 'Ancient Tree' before. It had been the last message on Primrose's computer; the friend that played the game with her and wanted her to meet him - the message sent by a man called Darius and it had caused Violette to act so strangely.

Looking at the panel once more, Elina knew for certain that Violette had not been telling the truth, and that she was responsible for whatever was imprisoned behind that door. Violette was also the one person responsible for Primrose's behaviour. In Elina's opinion, Primrose had never been troublesome, just misunderstood and unloved.

Violette, though, had tried hard to keep Primrose's talents hidden. Every time Primrose succeeded in something and photographs were taken, she feared it would attract the attention of Nastarana; the man Violette was trying desperately to shield her from. As Primrose grew so did her likeness to Briony, so much so that Violette had even taken a pair of scissors to her beautiful, golden hair and given her a spiky, boyish look. It was just a shame Violette was no hairdresser!

19. A STRANGE MEETING

'Arvensis, she's coming. Primrose is using meditation,' Forrestiana called out.

Forrestiana could not believe how excited she had become, she had hoped Primrose would have the intelligence to work out how to teleport, but had not realised how quickly she would achieve it. Finally, her dreams stood a chance of success.

Hurriedly, they made their way to the Circlet, excited at last to meet one of their grandchildren.

Within the Circlet, they caught their first glimpse of their eldest grandchild. The love they felt for her surprised them both, and they could barely contain their happiness. However, they were acutely aware that to Primrose they were both strangers and they would have to earn her trust. Primrose was just about to make the acquaintance of ghosts, it would not be something she would be expecting either.

As Primrose's form materialised in front of them, they marvelled at her composure and confidence.

Primrose felt the air around her crackle. It seemed charged with static electricity and it tingled gently against her skin. The hair on her arms tickled and stood on end. She noticed a circle start to form around her feet; it was marked with unfamiliar symbols. Scented candles on tall candlesticks flickered gently on the edge of the circle, casting many shadows. The smell of roses filled the air. Outside the circle there was nothing but darkness. Primrose stood in the middle circle of the Circlet.

Two indistinct, white figures stayed within the shadows, not wishing to alarm Primrose with their ghostly forms. Primrose noticed one was tall and broad shouldered with muscular arms that were folded across his chest; two silver gauntlets adorned his wrists and caught the flickering candlelight. Next to him stood a slim woman, dressed in a long, white gown, who was just as tall as the man. Primrose could see no more. She felt no fear; she sensed their excitement and curiosity. Primrose faced the man, looked him directly in the eyes and spoke confidently:

'Is my mother here?'

Arvensis was amused. Primrose had not asked the question; she had demanded it. Primrose was then slightly disconcerted as it was the woman that answered her question. Forrestiana was the matriarch of the peaceful souls that lived in the Sanctum.

'Unfortunately, your mother is still in the process of healing and cannot be present. The shock of this encounter could prove too much for her at present.'

'How do I know you speak the truth?' Primrose spoke defiantly, turning towards Forrestiana.

'You don't,' Forrestiana replied, using the same tone that Primrose had used, 'but you already know you can or you would not be here.'

Primrose chuckled inwardly; the response was one she would have probably used herself. Arvensis smiled and winked at her. Primrose had an uncanny feeling that he was reading her thoughts. Arvensis nodded. Primrose stared at him challengingly, but his smile touched her heart. Nevertheless, she tried to block her thoughts and feelings. It was too soon to form any emotional attachments.

'When the pair of you have finished weighing each other up, perhaps we can get down to business. What assistance do you require, Primrose?' Forrestiana asked.

Primrose once again looked straight at Forrestiana. She exuded power, confidence and magic. She was not surprised that they knew her name, she thought they might even know why she was here, but she thought it would be best to ask, just to be polite if nothing else.

'We believe the Ancient Tree has a lodger, Elina is convinced that whatever it is means us no harm, but it is close to death.'

The two shadowy figures conversed quietly for a moment; Primrose tried to use her magic and listen in to their conversation but found it had been blocked. Forrestiana turned and faced Primrose and spoke quickly and seriously.

'You were right to come here. Tell Elina not to worry and that you are going to disappear for a while. We need to speak with you privately. After speaking to Elina, press the rose on your bracelet and turn it anti-clockwise until it clicks. We need to be so careful. It is secure here.'

After warning Elina she was going to disappear, Primrose re-materialised in exactly the same spot.

Both figures stayed in the shadows. Feeling a wave of anger, Primrose stamped her foot.

'This is unfair, I've shown you some trust and you still remain partly hidden from me. Why?'

'She has a point,' Arvensis said.

'She has a quick temper too,' Forrestiana remarked, 'it needs controlling.'

'She has ears too!' Primrose snapped.

Arvensis laughed loudly, 'My, how she reminds me of you, my love - spirited and absolutely gorgeous.'

'You making fun of me?' Primrose asked, glaring at him.

'Not at all, it has been a long time since we have heard such outspoken honesty,' Arvensis replied and then became serious. He looked at his wife, and she nodded. Holding out his hand towards Primrose, he stepped inside the Circlet and his ghostly form materialised.

'Welcome to our home, oh granddaughter mine. We have waited a long time for this moment. I do not know about you, but I would dearly love a hug.'

'Can ghosts hug?' Primrose asked curiously, staring at him intently. She was not at all scared; this surprised her a bit, never having seen a ghost before.

'Time to find out,' Arvensis replied with a broad smile.

Primrose, without realising it, had taken the strong, spectral hand offered to her and quickly found herself hugged for the first time in... in fact, she could not remember the last time. She decided to just enjoy the feeling of comfort, and much to her disgust, Primrose felt her body give way to years of anguish; the arms wrapped around her tightened. She was not told to shut up or to get a grip or man up - her grandfather just let her be and do exactly what she needed to do.

After a while, as her sobs lessened, Primrose felt a feather-light touch brush the back of her head and she was turned and engulfed in the arms of Forrestiana, her grandmother. The love she felt and the comfort that flooded through her, healed her soul. Primrose felt true happiness.

'I'm sorry your mother cannot be here to greet you,' Forrestiana said soothingly, she held Primrose's face between her hands and looked directly into her tearful eyes, 'but she still needs to rest.'

As she finished speaking, she gently kissed Primrose's forehead. The kiss felt as delicate as a feather.

'Now to business,' Forrestiana said, her tone changing abruptly, 'What can we do to help you?'

Noting Primrose stiffen slightly, she added seriously, 'There will be other times for questions and answers, Primrose, but there are far more urgent things to be taken care of first, and your lodger is one of them.'

Primrose turned to her grandfather, who spoke straight away and just as seriously, 'I'm with your grandmother on this one, Primrose. We have not got time to waste. Come, tell us why you and Elina need our help.'

Primrose spoke honestly and clearly about her experiences with the panel, the energy she had felt and of the fear she had felt regarding the pull on her left hand. She then described Elina's vision and reiterated that the life form was close to death. She needed to know the correct way to deal with the matter as she was unsure what she might unleash. As she spoke her grandfather left the Sanctum, after receiving some kind of unspoken message from her grandmother.

'Your grandfather has gone to collect a few things for me. Now, Primrose, I cannot stress how important it is for you and Elina to remain invisible at all times. At present you are both believed to be lost or dead within the forest. Many eyes are

170

searching for clues of your existence. There is great evil about that would dearly love to possess and control the magic that you and Elina have. If this happens, the world as you know it will end. We need to bide our time. We know that Violette has tried to poison the minds of others, but whoever controls her is much more powerful and stronger than you or Elina can ever imagine. At present, you are both too inexperienced to deal with the superior magic that threatens us.'

As Forrestiana spoke, she held Primrose's hands and gave them an occasional squeeze, especially when she felt Primrose was about to argue.

'Once, many years ago, your grandfather and I believed we were strong enough too. We were wrong, but now with yourself and Elina we will be in a much stronger position, but I stress, the 'will be' is in the future and not now. I tell you this so you take no unnecessary risks, maintain your studies, as you are at present and remain hidden. We are so proud of you both for the speed and accuracy you are displaying with your magic.' Her grandmother paused once more and took a deep breath.

'I tell you this, because of the problem you now face with your lodger, if Dark Magic is involved the importance of remaining hidden and careful is vital. I too have no idea what it could be. This problem needs to be dealt with as soon as possible, especially if it is Dark Magic emanating from the hole at the top of the tree. The centre of the markings on the panel will be the thinnest and weakest point. This is where you are to use just an index finger to create a small hole and ascertain what is hidden behind it. Using any more fingers could put you and Elina in great danger,' she warned, 'Dark Magic is extremely volatile if stored in great amounts.'

Her grandfather entered the circle and gave her a net made of the finest silver.

'Use this to contain any leakage,' Arvensis said, 'the silver gives you protection against any Dark Magic that could be present. Gold has also been woven into the mesh to enhance its powers. Once you and Elina have discovered what is on the other side you must trap it within its folds and send it back here.'

'One more thing, Primrose,' her grandmother said, 'the letter written to Elina needs to be destroyed. If that were to get into the wrong hands the consequences could be fatal. See, Primrose, even your mother has a way of not following orders and acting too rashly, just like someone else I now know!' she added looking straight at Primrose with a smile.

'But the letter helped both Lina and myself and gave us comfort,' Primrose protested, 'I don't want to destroy it.'

'Sometimes, Primrose we need to do things against our wishes,' her grandmother interspersed, 'Showing signs of grieving can give the appearance that evil has triumphed. If you were to go around with smiles on your faces when you have lost someone dear to you, it would awaken curiosity and that kind of attention would be dangerous to us. Rules are in place for a reason, especially here. Promise me you will destroy the letter.'

'I'll speak to Lina and tell her of the dangers. When it's destroyed, I'll let you know.'

'There is no need; we will know when it is done.'

'Finally, before you go back, along with the net, we need to give you this…' her grandmother paused as Arvensis placed a scarf into Primrose's hands. 'Your mother made this out of the love she held for you. It offers you protection and warns you of the presence of Dark Magic. It is a truly beautiful gift.'

'Elina told me that one had been made for me, but it had been lost.'

'We have our ways,' her grandmother smiled warmly at her, 'Now, Primrose, you need to return. Use your bracelet, press it; turn it clockwise until it clicks. Do the opposite to come back to us.'

'When do we...?' Primrose paused and looked at the net.

'Tonight, when you get back,' her grandmother answered.

'Time is of the essence,' her grandfather confirmed, 'we need to know as soon as possible what lurks there.'

Primrose was once more engulfed within a tight hug from both grandparents. If she had to describe the feeling, she would probably have said it was like being immersed inside cotton wool or candyfloss, but not as sticky!

As she faded, she thought she heard her grandfather's voice call out to her, warning her not to do anything rash. As though she would, she grinned to herself.

20. A BRUSH WITH THE ENEMY

Elina felt a pulse of energy and slowly Primrose re-emerged sitting in the rocking chair. She waited patiently and watched her sister come round from what appeared to be a deep sleep. She sensed the mixed feelings of sadness, happiness, apprehension and excitement that Primrose had had to deal with.

'That was one roller-coaster trip of emotions,' Primrose admitted stroking Dilly, who had been trying hard to get her attention. 'I met our ghostly ancestors. Actual ghosts! Lina, they were wonderful, so loving. Grandmother is a sharp one. Between the two of us we should be able to wrap Grandfather around our little fingers.'

'And Mother?' Elina asked, desperate for news.

'Healing,' Primrose answered honestly, 'unable to be present this time.'

Elina watched Primrose as she paused for a moment, she felt she was about to hear something unpleasant. Her heart sank at the thought it could be bad news concerning their mother.

'I have three things to tell you, well four really. The first one is this,' Primrose said and pulled out the scarf that Briony had made her. It was the first time she had seen the scarf properly.

The delicately embroidered primroses in so many colours interspersed with green leaves took her breath away. Her mother had made this intricate, delicate, magical scarf just for her. She brought it to her face and breathed in deeply. For a moment, she thought she was going to cry again.

Elina crossed the room and placed her arms around Primrose's shoulders, and whispered in her ear, 'You're supposed to wear it, not eat it.'

Primrose gave a weak laugh and wrapped the scarf lovingly around her neck.

'And the second thing?' Elina queried.

'We have got to destroy your letter. If its read by our enemies it could give them too much information that could be fatal for us all. I intend to destroy the one that was left to me as well. I won't put our ancestors at risk, even if I'm not sure how you can put ghosts in danger. Lina, do you agree?'

Hearing the serious tone in Primrose's voice, Elina reluctantly agreed. Her scarf vibrated warmly against her skin and she knew she had chosen to do the right thing.

Primrose removed the letters from the cradle's secret drawer and placed them on the stove, ordering them to be destroyed by fire. The Ancient Tree obliged, the ashes then crumbled into miniscule pieces and disappeared.

The smell of roses filled the room and both girls understood the message.

'And the third?' Elina asked.

'Your bracelet is the way to teleport to our ancestors. If you are in danger you need to press the rose, turn it anticlockwise until it clicks and whoosh, away you go,' Primrose added dramatically, grinning, 'the reverse actions will bring you back. You might need to use the bracelet tonight.'

'What?' Elina exclaimed.

'That's the fourth thing I need to speak to you about,' Primrose said, enjoying the look of confusion on her sister's face. She produced the fine silver mesh from a deep pocket. 'We need to find out who our lodger is and take it to them.'

Primrose went on to explain about the magic contained in the silver mesh and of its protective qualities. She then outlined the plan of action that their grandmother felt would be the best way forward.

Elina practised pressing and moving the rose on her bracelet, without making it click and then tried and perfected the casting of the silver mesh, not wanting there to be a problem, when ensnaring whatever was imprisoned inside the Tree.

For a brief moment, she wondered if she should tell Primrose about the last text message she had received when staying at Violette's but then thought better of it. Primrose had enough on her mind without the added pressure of knowing that she could be dealing with someone she might have once known.

Both girls made an extremely big fuss of Dilly and Shadow, then briefed them as to what dangers they might be placing them into, yet again. If things were to go badly, the wolves were to meet them in the glade where Primrose had met Dilly. They were also told there might be a possibility that both Elina and Primrose could disappear suddenly and that they should not panic, because they were off to see Briony.

Elina made sure the trap door was open in case they or the wolves needed to make a quick getaway.

Walking towards the panel, they both took a deep breath and looked into each other's eyes.

'Ready?' Primrose asked.

'Ready,' Elina replied.

Primrose closed her eyes and placed her index finger in the middle of the strange markings on the panel, just as Forrestiana had told her.

Behind her, Dilly stood waiting with Shadow next to her, both ready to fight whatever might come through that panel. Elina held the fine silver net ready to use it for containment or as a barrier against evil.

Primrose felt the Gold Magic surge through her, down her finger and through the panel. Nothing happened. She withdrew her finger, breathed deeply and tried again, but still nothing happened. The accumulated Dark Magic on the other side of the panel was blocking her magic.

'It's not working,' Primrose said with frustration, drawing her brows together, clearly puzzled.

'Is your mind clear of fear?' Elina suggested, tongue in cheek.

'I must admit to feeling a teeny bit on edge,' Primrose laughed nervously.

'Could you try two fingers?'

'No, Grandmother said one should give enough leverage to start a dialogue with whatever is on the other side of this panel, two might...' Primrose let the sentence drift away, she would not think negatively.

'Try once more. If that doesn't work, perhaps I can channel some more energy through you as well. You know I'm a little bit more patient than you.'

'Are you saying that I might just blow it or us up? Don't

you trust me, Lina?' Primrose grinned. She had been thinking of ignoring her grandmother's advice, but the matriarch had unnerved her slightly. She was definitely not one to flaunt too many times.

'But the net?' Primrose queried, 'You need to be ready to use that with both hands.'

'We'll have to be resourceful,' Elina answered, 'Dilly and Shadow can help with that. They like a challenge.'

She turned and faced the young wolves, who wagged their tails happily; they would gladly do anything for either of them.

'One more try then. What are the magic words?' Primrose joked, 'Abracadabra or Open Sesame!'

'Try please,' Elina laughed, their nerves beginning to get the better of them.

'Still not working,' Primrose sighed with disappointment.

Elina stepped forward and gently placed her index finger on the back of Primrose's wrist, 'Try now,' she said seriously. Both girls locked eyes, smiled at each other and grinned. What could possibly go wrong?

'Something's happening, I think we're through.' Primrose exclaimed, as she felt a small vibration and heard a loud crack.

Elina and Primrose quickly moved away, as a small waft of black dust floated through the tiny hole created by their magic. Primrose clapped her hands together, muttered a few words and small burning embers sparkled briefly, then disappeared. With the dust dispersed safely, Elina quickly and efficiently placed part of the silver net over the hole, to protect themselves.

Dilly and Shadow still stood poised and ready for action.

At first Darius was confused; he thought he had heard a slight tapping and then a loud crack came from part of the wall that used to be a door, a noise that momentarily shattered his quiet world; a noise that had not been heard for a very, long time. He stared at the wall and saw a small pin-prick of light. He blinked; it was still there! Freedom! A chance of freedom had finally come to him. Tears streamed down his face. Hope blossomed.

'I don't think so. You're mine. Revenge will be ours. Remember what Lettie did to you. She needs to pay.'

'Go away!' he shouted loudly, 'I will not be taken. I will be free.'

However, reality struck, his hope quelled as he suddenly realised that he might inadvertently be putting another life in danger. But surely, he owed it to himself to make one last bid for freedom.

'Keep fooling yourself, my friend. I am coming. I have been patient for far too long!'

Primrose and Elina looked at each other.

'Did it tell us to go away?' whispered Elina, moving her ear closer to the hole.

Primrose tried to peer through the hole, but it was far too small. 'Who are you?' she asked softly.

'Move… escape… too much danger… for you. You need to go,' Darius's voice crackled, due to its lack of use; he had made the decision that he had no right to put another life at risk. It was her choice to make. 'You are too late!' he called out, resigned to his fate.

'Not a chance,' Primrose said confidently, 'not until you tell me who you are.'

'Stupid, silly child, go away!' Darius snapped; anger

mounting as he breathed in the dust created by the hole and realised that he was speaking to a young girl. He knew time was not on his side.

'*I am so close. You have not got a chance. Give in now. I will be gentle. Fight me and you will regret it!*'

'Idiot, go! You have no idea what trouble you are in!' Darius snapped again.

'Never been afraid of a bit of trouble - I'm not moving,' Primrose remarked calmly. 'Used to drive my mother mad, never did as she told me either, even when she asked nicely, which was rare. So what chance have you got, when I don't even know you.'

'You don't stand a chance, just go and do it quickly. Something is coming. I don't know what, but it's dangerous.' The effort of talking was tiring Darius; his throat was dry and parched. He hacked violently. 'You are too inexperienced to help. It's too late. Just go!'

'You'll be surprised just how much growing up I've done lately,' Primrose returned as she heard another vicious bout of coughing. After it ceased she stated firmly, 'Name first!'

'Then you must go,' Darius emitted a loud sigh, too tired to argue with the persistent child. At least some of his family might get to know what had become of him.

'Promise,' Primrose crossed her fingers; she would go, but only far enough to let Elina try to persuade the man to talk.

'Darius,' he answered, 'now go and be quick about it, there's too much danger approaching for you to stay any longer.'

Primrose could not believe it; she once had a gaming partner called Darius. She silently indicated to Elina to take her place and keep talking.

Darius, on the other hand, cursed his bad luck, but he would not sacrifice the girl, whoever she was. Too much guilt weighed on his conscience already; he would not be the cause of anyone else's suffering and have them endure the horrors he had been forced to.

A dark shape started to form on the edge of the forest, that to many looked like a small rain cloud. It began to snake its way sinisterly towards the Ancient Tree.

'Darius,' a new voice spoke to him, 'Primrose and I have no intention of leaving you in there. My mother would never forgive me or her. So help us out, we would dearly love to free you and send you somewhere safe, but we desperately need your co-operation.'

Darius was stunned; many years ago he'd had niece called Primrose. He glanced up at the dead computer, but the memory flitted away. He heard the new voice again; it was much softer than the first girl's. Once more he begged:

'You both need to go. Something is on its way. It will threaten you as well, if you don't run now. You have no idea what you are dealing with or the danger you are in.'

'If that's the case, you best start helping us then because we are an extremely stubborn duo, and we won't be going anywhere without you,' Elina spoke sternly and quickly.

'I can see the Ancient Tree! You will soon be mine for the taking.'

'I hope from your silence you are coming to the decision to co-operate. I hope so, because if something is on the way we don't have much time. As my mother would say, 'never give up' and the Ancient Tree would never forgive us. It told us you were here.'

No, no, no Darius thought. He knew that phrase, his sister Briony always said that to him, especially when he found things too hard and wanted to give up. Another niece, he thought. If this was correct then these two girls could possess magic and with the backing of the Ancient Tree he had a real chance of freedom.

'Freedom will be so much nicer with me, just let yourself go...'

Darius snapped his fingers, and the darkness shrunk slightly. He needed to get out of here and now; he needed to save these two girls.

'Inside the Ancient Tree there should be a belt, forest scenes, a silver clasp...' Darius spoke urgently. Primrose was already flying up the stairs; she knew exactly what belt he referred to, '... two diamonds; bring it. Widen the hole, pass it through. Then protect the hole with silver and Gold Magic if possible. Seal it forever with me in it. Too much Dark Magic in here: it will taint you. I will do the rest, as long as I have the belt.'

'Primrose knows of the belt you speak of and she has gone to retrieve it. She won't be long.'

'Who are you?' Darius called out.

'My parents are called Briony and Jack. My name is Elina,' Elina looked behind her as she heard a noise; Primrose breathing hard had skidded into the room, the belt held safely in her hands.

'We have the belt and the silver and the magic,' Elina exclaimed with relief, 'are you strong enough to activate the belt yourself, or shall we do it for you?'

'I have to press both diamonds,' Darius said, relieved that finally escape was within his grasp.

'Remember, keep positive. Don't give up. We will seal the hole this side once you have the belt, but we need to widen it first. Take a deep breath on our signal and try not to breathe in any more of that dust,' Elina ordered. 'Primrose and I know from experience how deadly that can be.'

'That I don't need to be told,' Darius laughed for the first time in years.

I'm here too...

Darius snapped his fingers and used the last of his Gold Magic, stalling the Darkness once more.

'Hurry, it's here, I've not got much time,' he begged.

'Breathe!' the two girls shouted.

Elina and Primrose moved quickly, reading each other's thoughts. They both knew they were up against the clock. The hole was widening; the girls used the same technique as before. They were nearly ready to pass the belt through, when they too heard the words, 'I'm here too.'

Darius convulsed as the dust thickened. His feet kicked madly at the walls of his prison. Black dust covered and enveloped him and darkness filled the small hole at the top of the cupboard, blocking out all light.

Mine!

'Go, Shadow. Go, Dilly. Go from the Tree.' Elina shouted at both wolves.

Both girls took a quick, deep breath of fresh, clean air and without further hesitation, they surged power at the small hole and blasted their way through it, momentarily halting the threatening darkness and buying a few more precious seconds. Wood splintered; dust billowed like an angry, storm cloud.

Elina shook out the silver net, and swept it around Primrose and herself. In the same moment, Primrose dispersed as much of the black, choking dust as possible with a sweeping spell and both girls dived onto the writhing form of Darius, still holding their breath.

Primrose placed the belt in Darius's right hand, placed one of his fingers on each of the diamonds and then covered them with her own. Elina sealed the silver net around them all; then she quickly turned the rose on her bracelet, before the net could slip.

Primrose pressed Darius's fingers onto the diamonds of his belt and successfully used a mind transference spell, for the first time, to turn her rose.

Both Elina and Primrose tried hard to hold the writhing body of Darius, which had become empowered by the evil contained within the inhaled dust. Elina channelled her magic into his struggling body and sent him into a deep sleep. As he relaxed, they hoped that the silver net would protect them all.

They landed heavily on a marble floor in the middle of the Circlet.

Back at the Ancient Tree, a chain reaction was set in motion. The Gold Magic used by both Primrose and Elina battled decades of accumulated, ingrained, dark dust that plastered the walls of that ridiculously small room. The resulting explosion could be heard miles away. As it reverberated loudly throughout the dark forest, it snapped branches off of trees and made the leaves billow into the air.

A salvo of explosions sent burning splinters of wood soaring into the air like fireworks. They exploded noisily and violently; spraying golden particles into the night's sky and forming a fantastic display of power and light. Eventually, the embers floated harmlessly down to earth like soft, glittering snowflakes.

Shadow and Dilly had heard the serious, imperative tone in Elina's voice and had reacted immediately to her orders. Both wolves realised that they had decided to do something extremely dangerous; it was a command neither dared to disobey and one they knew they had to adhere to immediately.

The two young wolves ran for their lives, as jagged splinters of wood zeroed in on them like guided missiles. They swerved behind trees, boulders and any object that could deflect or give protection from the lethal shrapnel that followed them. Eventually they had covered enough distance to ensure their safety and they slowed their pace to a trot. Both wolves, thankfully, escaped without serious injury.

Finally, Dilly and Shadow stopped. They turned back to look at the Ancient Tree and saw that one massive branch was missing. It had been cleaved explosively from the immense trunk and totally obliterated.

But, most amazing of all, the Tree had already started the process of healing itself. Slowly the splintered, jagged scar caused by the explosion changed back to old bark, in front of their eyes. The Ancient Tree finally free of the Darkness that had slowly been spreading its poison began to blossom for the first time in years.

Both wolves wondered if their mistresses had been as lucky as they had been and hoped they were both safe and sound. Together they began their trek to the forest glade where Dilly and Primrose had first met, anxious for news. Behind them an ominous, shadowy form retreated and returned from whence it came, frustrated that he had played his game for far too long and allowed too much Dark Magic to build up within the Ancient Tree.

21. A HOME-COMING

In the middle of the Circlet, Primrose and Elina rolled out from beneath the silver net giggling hysterically, their nervous energy and excitement dissipating with laughter. Each checked the other over meticulously, they were totally unharmed.

The stern faces of Forrestiana and Arvensis stared down at them.

'Of all the stupid, silly, reckless, pranks to play...' Forrestiana burst out.

'Never seen the like, to risk your lives...' Arvensis called out loudly.

Primrose and Elina grinned at each other and carefully, very carefully, lifted a tiny corner of the net to reveal the withered, emaciated body of Darius. They quickly re-covered the figure with the silver net to keep contamination to a minimum.

Shock registered on the faces of Forrestiana and Arvensis, as they suddenly recognised the distorted, wasted face of their son. They shook their heads in total disbelief.

'Darius,' Forrestiana whispered aloud, 'we were told he was dead.'

Silent tears started to fall from her eyes, as she stood and stared at the shape of her son still lying unconscious under the protection of the silver net.

'I think he still breathes, but he has taken in so much Dark Magic and needs your help,' Primrose said softly with concern, looking directly at her grandparents.

'I used a comatose spell to help him sleep and relax. He was extremely difficult to hold down,' Elina explained apologetically, nervously looking around her. She recognised no one and felt that at any moment she would be blamed for the state of the man they had just rescued.

Arvensis took one look at his grief-stricken wife and galvanised everyone into action. Orders were given and carried out quickly and efficiently. Both Elina and Primrose were ordered to be cleansed of all the black dust that could still be clinging to their clothes and bodies. Afterwards their minds were to be scanned. It was hoped that they might have observed something that could reveal some clue as to what had happened to Darius.

Elina had no time to take in all the unusual spectral sights of her ancestors' home. She was efficiently swept away, along with Primrose for cleansing, by someone they later came to know as Umbro, the Alchemist.

Meanwhile, Darius was placed into the immediate care of Solis, the Healer. His frail body was sealed more carefully within the silver mesh. Magical spells eliminated all traces of contamination and a shimmering, golden halo of protection and healing was created around him.

Gently and reverently Arvensis lifted his son from the floor, to take him to a room where the healing process would continue.

As Arvensis felt the incredible lightness of his son's form, he battled to control the anger that surged and boiled within him. He longed to remove the silver gauntlets from his wrists and blast his own Dark Magic towards the evil that had caused this, but he knew that would be a terrible mistake.

Many years ago, he had used his magic unwisely and because of his lack of patience, his stubbornness and overconfidence he had made a bad situation worse, and played straight into his brother's hands. He would not do it again. Forrestiana was right, they had to gather all intelligence, be prepared and wait. If his son could be saved, they would have a much stronger chance to overthrow his twin and his dream for his family to be reunited would finally come true. He just hoped his son's mind would be strong enough; he had suffered far too much and for too many years.

Forrestiana still stood in her original spot. She had cast her spells like some kind of automaton; her grief and anger red raw as she had looked on the lifeless form of her son. Suddenly, she spoke out loudly and harshly, 'She told me he was dead. How could she do that?'

22. ELINA MEETS HER GRANDPARENTS

Black dust eliminated and the cleansing rituals over, Elina stood and stared at the ghostly form of the tall man that faced her. She ignored his outstretched hand of welcome. She did not trust him, something oozed from his persona, something inexplicable. It unsettled her. She knew it was not because he was a ghost or her grandfather, but whatever it was made her feel extremely vulnerable. As he stepped forward, she stepped back and held both hands out to stop his advance; her mind commanded him to stay away from her.

'Being a bit dramatic, Lina,' Primrose remarked, amused at first by her reaction to her grandfather. 'He doesn't bite.'

'But he has the ability to,' Elina replied more sharply than she had intended. She was trying hard to understand the strange feeling of uncertainty she felt towards him. Arvensis had allowed her to probe his mind to some extent regarding his feelings towards her. She sensed his love and sorrow at her continued rejection, but something sinister lurked within him, and it wasn't the Dark Magic that he possessed.

Arvensis was not going to deny it, but as he watched his youngest granddaughter's continuous scrutiny, witnessed her stubbornness and lack of trust, he felt a deep pain in his heart, the like he had never felt or experienced before. He continued to allow her to search parts of his mind in the hope it would give her a sense of his character, hoping she would come to trust him, but it had not helped. She had become even more wary. Her eyes mirrored her confusion and reminded him of a startled deer.

He was amazed at the strength of Elina's magic; it was surprisingly strong given her youth and inexperience, especially as it had been achieved without the aid of a tutor.

Elina's type of magic was extremely rare. This moment, he felt sure, she sensed parts of his past that flamed her distrust of him. He had not seen a novice of this quality in decades, a soul that could see and predict both the past and the future - a Sentient. She was a soul to be cherished, but it was her love and trust that he wished to gain, and he hoped fervently that she would give him both.

Elina relaxed slightly; she had been reading his thoughts as clearly as if he had spoken, but she was not yet ready to give in to him.

'Tell me! What is it about you that I don't understand?' she finally demanded.

Her grandfather smiled, what was it about these grand-daughters of his? Their first sentences uttered to him were more of a demand than a simple question. Life had certainly become more interesting since the pair of them had entered the Ancient Tree.

'Do I not get even a please or just a hint of a warm welcome?' he asked gently, and was further amused to see a look of frustration and a hint of annoyance cross her face.

'For the love of peace, Arvensis, tell her what it is that puzzles her or we will be here all night.'

A tall figure had entered the room; Elina recognised the family connection immediately and sensed the authority the woman carried as well as the power of the magic she possessed. She knew immediately it was her grandmother. As a ghost, Forrestiana was still a striking woman and her presence automatically commanded respect and trust.

'What is it with you and these granddaughters of yours? A warm welcome is what they require, not a show down!'

'It's a man thing,' Arvensis replied.

'It is the wrong thing,' Forrestiana retorted.

'You know it is my intention to have the first hug from both of my granddaughters, oh wife of mine.'

Primrose responded immediately. Her second hug that night from her grandfather was medicine to her soul. Elina, on the other hand, walked sedately towards Forrestiana; her grandmother's resemblance to Briony was both uncanny and comforting. It was just the hug and reassurance she desperately needed after the death of her mother.

As her grandmother released Elina from her embrace, Elina once more turned towards her grandfather.

'Well?' she asked stubbornly.

Her grandfather raised an eyebrow. He had just received yet another demand, but he smiled gently at her.

'Please,' Elina added.

'You sense my evil twin, but as long as I wear these… everyone is totally safe,' he replied seriously, indicating the gauntlets that covered the back of his hands and lower arms and raising them in the air. 'Now, can I have at least a shake of the hand, if not a hug.'

Arvensis' smile widened as he read the expression on Elina's face and saw her finally make sense of the confusion that had troubled her earlier. Once more he held out his hand. Elina took it hesitantly and was swept into the tightest of ghostly hugs.

'Now to business,' Forrestiana said, her tone changing and becoming serious, 'It will be sometime before Darius, our son, will be able to communicate. At present he needs intensive nursing and sleep.' A note of irritation or anger sounded momentarily in her voice. 'We might even have to fabricate a special room if he feels threatened by suddenly having too much space, but we will cross that bridge when or if it happens. But now, I need to find out how far your learning has progressed by searching your minds. At the same time I will look for clues concerning the current danger that faces us, and of any knowledge that you hold in your psyche.'

Forrestiana held up her hands as she saw that both Elina and Primrose were about to protest.

'There is to be no argument, the process is harmless and takes a matter of seconds. There is nothing to be scared of and it will be easier to do if I have your full co-operation.'

'First, I need to know if it is possible to see my, our,' Elina glanced quickly at Primrose and gave her an apologetic smile, 'our mother tonight?' The request was made quietly but seriously, 'I believe it is essential that we do.'

Forrestiana raised her eyebrows, 'You have a feeling?' she queried.

'I believe she needs to hear or sense our forgiveness: it is slowing her recovery. The feeling of guilt overwhelms her soul. She cannot forgive herself for failing to recognise my magic or for her treatment of Primrose.'

Elina saw a transient flicker of refusal cross her grandmother's face, so added, 'I am aware of your need to protect her because of how fragile she is. I have sensed that since our arrival. Our mother can be asleep during our visit.'

'Very well, I will trust in your instinct, but she is my daughter and I only want what is best for her - to protect her from further harm. A false memory could cause a set-back in her recovery. Now, I need both of you to follow me back to the Hall and the Circlet.'

Once inside the Circlet, Elina was invited to enter the central circle; burning candles encircled both her and her grandmother. Her grandmother gently placed a hand on each side of Elina's head and closed her eyes. Elina felt a mild fuzziness and a slight tingle as her head was released.

'Is that it?' she asked, surprised just how quick the process had been.

'All completed,' Forrestiana confirmed.

'Couldn't have been much inside that head of yours, Lina,' Primrose joked, as she looked inside one of her sister's ears and waved her hand on the other side of Elina's head, 'Yep, nothing there, I can see my other hand.'

Forrestiana gave Primrose a stern look, being unaccustomed to humour. Her life had been too serious for too long. She invited her to step forward and the process was repeated and accomplished just as quickly.

Motioning the girls to follow her, their grandmother left the

Sanctum. Neither Elina nor Primrose spoke: they sensed the seriousness of their grandmother's mood and followed suit.

For the first time, they were able to take in their surroundings. They were being led along a white marble corridor with marble pedestals topped with cut-glass, and crystal vases that were filled with scented roses of various colours. Silver sconces adorned the walls and twinkled merrily as the candles inside lit their way. Their grandmother paused outside a white, oak door with an elaborate carving that showed two adult wolves.

'Luna,' Primrose squealed with delight, 'I stroked that wolf years ago. Briony... no, my mother took me to see her. If I remember right her mate's name was Sirrus or something similar.'

'Sirius,' Elina corrected, remembering the entry in Primrose's diary. They were both aware that they stood outside their mother's room.

'Sweet Briar does not look as you would expect,' their grandmother warned. 'Here, when you pass over and become a Peaceful Soul you can choose a 'look' from any age of your past. You may go in. I will be back soon and we will speak again before you return to the Ancient Tree.

23. BRIONY

Quietly and carefully, Elina opened the door and softly they both crossed the room and looked down at the sleeping form of their mother. Briony had chosen to be in her twenties. Her youthful face was framed with translucent curls. She looked both familiar and unfamiliar at the same time. It felt as though they stood and stared at an older sister rather than their mother. It was a strange feeling. Elina had never known her mother look this young and she felt strangely alienated from her.

Gently lifting her mother's hand from the bed, she felt its warmth and then the connection. Bending slowly she placed a gentle kiss on each cheek and then rubbed noses softly - when she was younger it had been one of their bedtime rituals. She then whispered softly into her mother's ear.

'It's Elina, mother, I love you. I am fine and have made friends with Primrose. There is nothing to forgive. Resurgam.' She gently replaced her mother's hand onto the duvet, stepped back and allowed Primrose to greet her real mother for the first time.

'She has the same hair style that I had before Violette cut it,' Primrose said, touching her own hair and her mother's. Elina saw a smirk lift the corners of Primrose's mouth; she recognised the sign; Primrose was up to something.

'When I was a kid,' Primrose said, 'Briony would let me do her hair. If I am ever so gentle…' Primrose leant forward and with a gentleness that she had not used for years, quickly and expertly created a single pigtail to hang over her mother's left ear. They smiled softly as they looked down on their mother.

'Do you think that's alright, Lina?' Primrose asked, suddenly feeling guilty, 'I don't want her to think I'm making fun of her. It's just something we used to enjoy doing; it would make us both laugh so much.'

'It's perfect, Primrose,' Elina remarked, 'It's just what she needs. It will spark a good memory, a sign that you remember the good times and that you care.'

Primrose bent over and placed a single kiss in the centre of her mother's forehead, 'Primrose says sorry, it has taken me awhile, but I sort of understand now. I love you.'

Gently she traced her index finger down her mother's cheek and then placed it to her own lips, before wiping a tear from her eye.

'Time to go,' Primrose said softly, reaching for her sister's hand, 'What did that Latin thing mean?'

'Resurgam - it means rise again; it was a word that she insisted father put on her coffin.'

As they gently opened the door, they heard their mother sigh in her sleep, 'I love you both too.'

24. THE HIDDEN DANGER EXPLAINED

Once outside and back in the corridor, their grandmother beckoned them towards another room. This time the door depicted a carving of a tree with a wild cat in its topmost branches spitting at a bear that stood on its rear legs.

'Which one do you think is Grandmother's familiar?' Primrose laughed, 'My money is on the wildcat, claws on the outside and a lovely kitty on the inside.'

Primrose was rewarded with another stern look from her grandmother, softened by a slight quirk that tugged at the corners of her mouth.

'Why not come in and ask?' she answered as she stepped aside and allowed both girls to enter.

The warmth, comfort and forest colours of the room were a stark contrast to the pristine whiteness of the corridor, but it was not the homeliness of the room that took the girl's breath away. It was the giant brown bear sprawled on its back in front of a blazing fire and the intense, yellow stare from the eyes of a wildcat, glaring at them from one of its many vantage points - a series of shelves set in the walls.

'Our familiars,' explained their grandfather, 'Meet Bruin and Felina. The wildcat is mine. She reminds me of someone,' he explained and grinned, looking directly at his wife, 'your description was quite apt, Primrose.'

'Make yourselves at home,' Forrestiana said, 'I am aware that you must be tired and hungry. You have both had an extremely long day, but I am afraid there is much to discuss and you need to return to your wolves as soon as possible.'

Primrose immediately made herself comfortable next to her grandfather. The wildcat hissed and purposefully unsheathed each of its front claws one by one and watched her intently. Primrose was sure that each sharp claw glinted especially for her as it expressed its displeasure at her seating choice.

'Are you going to call that cat off? I don't think she likes me,' Primrose remarked, staring back at the cat with equal dislike and distrust.

'Definitely not,' her grandfather replied smiling, 'competition is healthy, oh granddaughter mine.'

Elina sat down next to Bruin and gently began to stroke his belly, thinking of Shadow and Dilly. She knew their wolves were safe, but she also sensed their anxiety - they had begun to fret about their safety and absence.

Their grandmother snapped her fingers and a selection of sandwiches, savouries and cakes appeared before them. Also, much to Primrose's delight - hot chocolate drinks!

'It is just as well you decided not to eat the cake Violette gave you,' their grandmother remarked casually, 'I can assure you; these ones are perfectly safe.'

Elina looked puzzled for a moment, 'How did…?'

'Each soul here has a familiar, mine is Bruin, your grandfather's is the jealous wildcat over there and we also have a fox at the Sanctum. Foxes are secretive animals that love to forage and are extremely street-wise. It has followed you since your arrival at Violette's.'

'But Shadow would have told…'

'Shadow has been aware of him but he sensed, somehow, that the fox was of no threat. I would like to read his mind one day. I believe some of that gold dust you wafted around so freely when you brought Primrose back to life again may have had some bearing on his sensitivity.'

Elina was not sure whether her grandmother was rebuking her for a moment, but she noticed her expression soften.

'Shadow was close to all the action that day,' Forrestiana explained, 'and both wolves have been surrounded with much magic since then. They seem to have acquired some extraordinary powers of their own. I digress, the fox, or Reynard as we call him here, retrieved the remains of the cake from the bin. The black, gooey mess has been examined by our Alchemist, Umbro. He has identified most of the compounds, barring one substance. Its identification at present still eludes him, much to his annoyance. The cake also contained a powerful sedative. If you had eaten it, you would not be speaking with us now.'

'Instead,' her grandfather interspersed, 'we believe you would have been making the acquaintance of my evil twin, Nastarana, my nastier side.'

'So you know who threatens us,' Primrose spoke out, her excitement rising.

'We have known all along, oh granddaughter mine,' her grandfather said. 'My brother is a very powerful magician, stronger than us as we found out many years ago, but we now believe he has created something more sinister.'

'But you have Elina and me now,' Primrose said.

'We had older and more experienced magicians back then too and little good it did us,' her grandfather added. 'No, Primrose, we are still too weak and you still have a lot to learn. Furthermore, both of you are too inexperienced in battle. We must play a waiting game.'

'We could do with Evelyn,' their grandmother added sadly, 'We believe Violette not only swapped Darius's belt that night, but stole Evelyn's bracelet too. It is why she could not be located and brought here or brought herself. I fear she has been lost to us forever. After the Great Flood her bracelet was found washed up at our burial site and spotted by the keen sight of our kestrel, another familiar.'

'I think I might have met Evelyn, but I'm not sure,' Elina said.

'I sensed that too, when I read your mind, but I believe it to be an extremely, clever automaton and one to be extremely careful of. It is gaining the trust of too many,' her grandmother added sadly.

'An automaton?' both Elina and Primrose asked simultaneously.

'Nastarana, your grandfather's twin, uses robots in the form of cleverly shaped drones. These drones replicate the movements of animals and continually monitor the Ancient Forest,' Forrestiana explained. 'The last drone we discovered was an owl, a cleverly constructed long-eared owl. Its flight path was effortless and smooth, a brilliant piece of technology. It had one fault - its feathers never moved. Thank goodness our kestrel's keen eye-sight detected that flaw. Now, thanks to Elina's memory we know of another. Our familiars will be working extremely hard once more trying to locate it - a large bat that you spotted at the edge of the forest.'

Elina recalled the memory and knew that in future she should take more notice when something seemed odd or out of place. She needed to take heed of her sixth sense and act on it.

Changing the subject rather abruptly their grandfather spoke and brought the subject back to Evelyn.

'Our daughter had,' he then quickly corrected himself, he so much hoped she was alive, 'has lovely, brown eyes, with flecks of green in her right eye. She used to pretend that it was a spy camera that took secret photographs. If you see her again, examine the right eye. My brother might be extremely clever, but he has a tendency to ignore the smaller details and can be, at times, complacent, a weakness we hope to exploit in the future.' Their grandfather reminisced sadly. His family had been completely destroyed, one way or another by his twin. He felt useless trapped in this ghostly underworld.

Forrestiana continued, looking at Primrose, 'If Sweet Briar had not turned you to stone; Violette would have been persuaded eventually to deliver you into his hands as well.

'So, Lina and I have been destined to meet each other either way,' Primrose said thoughtfully, 'What part does Vile Vi play in all of this?'

'That is yet to be fully revealed,' their grandfather said. 'She has been known to help us, on rare occasions, as well as helping Nastarana. She could be playing her own game or being forced to play his. I believe and hope it is the former. I sometimes wonder if the cakes she sold from her company had a little extra something in them; that is why we need our Alchemist to discover what that elusive substance is.'

'I was hoping that Sharna would return with another sample. However, she has not been back since giving Violette an impromptu visit. I am finding her tardiness a little bit unsettling and hope nothing has happened to her.' Their grandmother spoke sadly. Elina sensed she was deeply troubled.

'Sharna?' Primrose asked.

'Your mother's familiar, a brown rat.'

'I've seen it!' Elina said excitedly.

'Classic! Vile Vi hates rats with a passion,' Primrose spoke out with a loud laugh.

'The night we left Violette's my scarf vibrated,' Elina said, 'at the time, I thought the way the rat looked at me was odd; it seemed to want to give me a message, but we were in such a rush to leave the apartment that I hastened Shadow away as quickly as possible.'

'Sharna would have been pleased to see you leaving, as it was the task she had been assigned to do,' her grandmother said.

'At rat helped me find my way into the Ancient Tree,' Primrose added, remembering the time she had nearly given up.

'Sharna also helped Dilly escape from a pack of wolves too,' Forrestiana remarked, 'She has been extremely helpful these last few weeks. On the subject of familiars, Bruin and Felina will be part of your next training sessions. Bruin and Felina are going to try and set up a territory in your part of the forest. I want Shadow and Dilly to try and chase them both away. They are to be part of a diversion I have in mind. As they run I want you to chase them with the orbs. This will help you practise all that you have learnt under more pressure, and at the same time, we can try and locate further automatons. Nastarana sends his drones out daily,' Forrestiana paused and turned towards Primrose.

'Primrose, you need to learn how to use the spheres when

they are outside your protective barrier, especially the black ones. Keep the barrier tight to you and do not let it impede your arm movements. You need to practice with the wind and the different elements that will affect the spheres' movements.

'Also, I want you and Elina to be creative in the making of them by using the magic you *both* possess and taking note of the various power combinations.

'As soon as we finish here, your grandfather is going to give you, Primrose, a quick practise session in how to tighten your protective barrier and improve your control of the orbs. I found it interesting to note that even Darius gave you a lesson or two in the art of stalking and observing the minute actions of your prey in order to capture them. However, in your case you liked to eliminate them.'

Primrose looked at her grandmother, positive that she had just received a slight rebuke from her.

'Are you talking about the computer game?' Primrose asked, momentarily confused how her grandmother had known about the game she had once played with Darius.

'I read your minds, remember,' their grandmother answered patiently. 'It has been really helpful putting different threads of your memories together with our intelligence. We believe Nastarana is preparing for another strike against us.'

Elina surprised everyone when she added, 'I believe it will be on the night of the next Full Moon. My father has convened another meeting to take place at our mother's resting place. There will be many present. I sense some sort of fire energy and lots of it.'

'Are you sure?' Arvensis asked, 'That place is situated above our heads. That would mean he is definitely going to try and destroy us again. Fire would make sense; he's tried air and water before. It also ties in with the Ancient Ballad's prediction.'

'Can't you just join us at the Ancient Tree?' Primrose suggested.

'We are not allowed above ground, unless certain criteria are completed or Ancient Laws are contravened,' Forrestiana explained.

'That's easy then. Lina and I will complete the criteria you speak of,' Primrose added, becoming excited.

'We do not have enough time, the moon is nearing its last quarter and unfortunately you lack the experience needed to complete all of the tasks,' her grandfather said.

Primrose felt her frustration rising and said loudly, 'Experience, experience, experience and the lack of it, that's all I keep hearing!'

'I am sorry, oh granddaughter mine, but if we act too rashly now we will never recover from the danger that threatens us.' Arvensis said, trying to calm Primrose. 'My brother's one big weakness is that he believes himself to be invincible. We need him to truly believe he has won and that none of us have survived. We have waited too long to jeopardise our plans at this stage.'

Elina, who had been sitting quietly, suddenly had an idea, 'If he is to act on the night of the Full Moon when we are all gathered together in one place, can we not bring the meeting forward a day? No one gets hurt that way.'

'But that just delays the inevitable and to an unknown time and that is even more dangerous.' Forrestiana said, 'At the moment we have the advantage, we know an attack is pending, and when. We also believe that Nastarana is also unsure whether we survived his previous attacks.'

'I believe Elina has a good point. If everyone meets on the eve of the Full Moon we will gain more time and Darius, Sweet Briar, Elina and Primrose will be more powerful with extra training from us,' Arvensis suggested.

'I need to think on it,' Forrestiana said, 'we could move to a safer place. It could buy us time and if he does strike here, he breaks the Ancient Laws again and then who knows what will happen…'

'What happened to you, why are you here?' Primrose asked.

Arvensis laughed. He had wondered when one of his grand-daughters would ask about them; it had taken them longer than he had expected. 'Many years ago, my brother Nastarana tricked us into a battle. It later became known as the Battle of the Roses, because of our names. As you may be aware all magicians are named after a rose. We obviously lost, and as a punishment he banished us here. However, as we turned our backs on him, he must have had a change of heart because he blasted us with a bolt of superheated air, believing that it would kill us outright.' Arvensis paused, remembering the moment.

'What Nastarana did not take into consideration were the Ancient Laws. In trying to kill us, he had broken them,' Forrestiana continued, 'We were allowed to live on as ghosts. The next time he tried to kill us was the night of the Great Flood. He wished to drown us; luckily for us the waters gave way too soon. That time, as the laws were broken again our magic was restored to us. However, if Sharna has been captured, he may now know where we are and also that you two have survived, as well as Violette's own child. The danger we face is very real.'

'Violette's daughter?' Primrose asked.

'Your mother saved her on the night of the flood.' Forrestiana explained, 'Hopefully, you can meet Villosa next time you come, but we need to get you back to the Ancient Tree soon, and Primrose, you need to work with your grandfather and perfect the use of those dark orbs. I will talk with Elina to try and find some ways of weakening Nastarana's magic. Now, I cannot stress how important it is for you both to remain completely invisible at all times, even if you were to meet your father again. It is vital that Jack gives no one any clue of your whereabouts. I still believe Nastarana has no idea where you are or how strong your magic has become, especially in such a short time. He would consider it incredible, therefore unbelievable.'

Forrestiana stopped speaking and exchanged a quick glance with Arvensis. Primrose noticed a small, nearly imperceptible shake of the head from her grandmother.

'What just happened then, don't you trust us?' Primrose asked with an edge to her voice.

'You are too sharp, oh granddaughter mine,' her grandfather replied, looking directly at Primrose, 'You may not like what just passed between us, but I will tell you nonetheless. Once Nastarana has destroyed this place, he will then destroy all other magical places and anyone who helped us.'

'Our tree!' Primrose called out as her grandfather's words sunk in.

'Our friends! The Cottage!' Elina moaned, 'Surely he wouldn't be so cruel as to kill the animals as well?'

'I am sorry, but yes,' Forrestiana answered regretfully.

'Well that's so not going to happen, I won't let it,' Primrose said firmly.

'There can be no other way,' Forrestiana said, 'Nastarana

needs to believe he has been successful, believe himself to be invincible, and more importantly be convinced that we are all dead.'

'Well, I will find a way to save the Ancient Tree, even if I have to create a special barrier. I will not let it die, not after what it has done for me,' Primrose declared.

Forrestiana remained silent; she knew it would be pointless arguing with Primrose. She looked at Arvensis as he quietly stood up, it was time for him to take Primrose's mind off of the Ancient Tree.

'Come, oh granddaughter mine, time for some action and practise. Come and take your frustrations out on me.'

Primrose left the room with her grandfather, while Elina remained with her grandmother to discuss all details and possibilities that might arise on the night before the Full Moon.

When Elina was sure that Primrose was out of earshot, she looked at her grandmother and whispered, 'Do you really think your wish is possible, if Nastarana tries to take your lives once more?'

Forrestiana's eyes narrowed and she looked sharply at Elina.

'I can read your mind. I saw your dream and hopes for the future,' she told her grandmother.

'But your magic is not strong enough to do that! For a magician of your age to be able to read the mind of a magician like me is unheard of, the last magician with that ability was Rosa Hugonis. Can I?' Forrestiana reached her hands towards Elina and gently placed her hands on her forehead once more to scan the depth of her magic.

'This is truly amazing. In fact, it is totally unbelievable. Your magic is incredibly strong. I was considering using Bruin to relay messages between us, but I now believe you and I will be able to communicate telepathically. It is another skill that you should not have. We can use it when you are above ground. What do you think, Elina?'

'It's definitely worth a try. Who was Rosa Hugonis?'

'An extremely powerful magician; he sacrificed his magic on the condition that all magicians and accomplices who survived the battle would be banished underground to this Sanctum. He saved four of us, but then Nastarana turned his magic on him as well. To this day we don't know what spell was cast on him.'

'Do you know what became of him? Is he a relation of mine?' Elina asked, Hugonis was her surname.

Forrestiana looked deeply into Elina's eyes and sighed deeply, 'He's your father, Elina. It is why the magic you both have is so special, combined with that of your mother's the possibilities and strength of what you both possess is unknown. Nastarana would dearly like to be able to control you both.'

Elina became very quiet as she thought over her grand-mother's words and was somehow not surprised to learn that her father had once possessed magic, but it was someone else her thoughts had turned to - Violette. She began to suspect that Violette might have been playing a very dangerous game. What if Violette knew of the danger that threatened both her and Primrose? Could that be the reason why she had allowed Primrose to be kept as a statue, protected by Briony's magic? Elina remembered her scarf had vibrated strangely in Violette's room the night she had left. The scarf had never vibrated in Violette's presence before, so what magic had been nearby that night, she wondered. Had Violette secretly warned her to leave?

'Now to business, how can we weaken Nastarana's magic?' Forrestiana said, interrupting Elina's thoughts.

'Slowly, bit by bit,' Elina stated, with no idea where that thought had come from.

Forrestiana and Elina conversed for another hour, discussing ideas and plans of what they believed could happen if the family were to face Nastarana on the night of the next Full Moon.

25. PRIMROSE'S FIRST LESSON WITH AN EXPERT

As they left the room, Primrose asked her grandfather why he wore the gauntlets.

'To keep everyone safe; oh granddaughter mine. My Dark Magic is very powerful and without these I would, in time, be just like my evil twin. They have been specifically designed for me; silver for everyone's protection and to keep me in touch with my softer side and emotions; pewter to control my energy and miniscule veins of gold to boost the powers of the metals.'

'And I thought you wore them just because they looked good,' Primrose joked.

Her grandfather smiled at her comment and opened a door, beckoning her inside. Primrose found herself inside a large underground cave. She had never seen anything like it before and marvelled at its beauty, but her grandfather gave her no time to admire her surroundings - she was here to learn.

The cave was lit with many flickering candles that shone off the wet walls that were coloured in many shades of orange. From the ceiling hung wonderful formations of stalactites and from the floor stalagmites stretched majestically towards their hanging cousins. Deep pools mirrored the light and the ceiling, giving the illusion of unknown depths and dangers.

True to his word, Primrose was shown how to tighten her shield around her body to maintain both her invisibility and safety. Afterwards, she was shown how to create the smallest of black, magical orbs which resembled grains of rice but still packed a powerful punch. Her grandfather then made his own orbs and sent them spinning and skidding around the cave, weaving them skilfully around the fantastic rock formations and across still pools of water, enhancing the optical illusion of depth and danger. Primrose watched spellbound as she studied his movements closely.

'Stop gawking and chase my spheres with your own,' he ordered in a tone not to be argued with.

For the next few minutes, with Primrose's skill improving, she managed to hit just one of his orbs. She believed it to be by pure luck, as she cut off its course when it spun round one of the cave's formations. She waited nervously for the impending explosion, but none came, and her hesitation made her lose all of her orbs to her grandfather.

'Where my brother is concerned, there can be no hesitation. One moment's loss of concentration and you are…'

Suddenly, Primrose found herself the target of all her grandfather's orbs and had to dodge, jump and run to avoid them.

'Not fair…' she screamed at him.

'Nothing is fair in war. Fight back Primrose. Darius taught you better than to run.'

'But, this is … ow… not a… ow… computer… ow…game!'

'Then make it one!' he laughed back at her. 'If you are going to use magic, you need to know what it feels like too.'

It was the laugh that did it. Primrose would have no one laugh at her, not any more. She tightened her shield, surprised by how much she had allowed it to weaken. She had been too concerned about the explosions that never materialised.

Primrose made several of her own orbs. Her grandfather's orbs were now bouncing quietly off her shield and disintegrating, without a single flash.

Now that she felt more confident, and knew there would be no explosions, Primrose was able concentrate and go in for the attack, even though she knew there could be a possibility of gaining a few more painful bruises.

'Well done, oh granddaughter mine, I commend your spirit. Aim for me.'

Her grandfather did not let up. He forced her to maintain her shield and control her orbs while under continuous fire. She had never felt so exhilarated, so engrossed and so energised, but so frustrated at the same time. Then she remembered something Darius had told her - if she was not making progress through a level, she needed to examine her technique and change tactics.

Primrose gathered all her orbs together to change her attack; her grandfather disappeared. She spun around quickly but he was gone.

'Ow!' she cried, as another orb smashed into her; once again she had let her shield weaken.

'You were too easy to read, if you change tactics, so do I,' he goaded her.

Primrose nearly stamped her foot in annoyance as she tightened her shield once more, but this time she closed her mind to all thoughts, except for the space she was in. She secretly praised her grandfather for making her think much harder and testing her skills more thoroughly, but chided herself for continually letting her shield weaken.

With amazing speed Primrose fired all her orbs together and outwards in every direction in a vicious salvo. They ricocheted off the cavern walls, bounced off the stalactites and criss-crossed the cave like an intricate spider's web.

She heard a surprised cry from her grandfather and danced ecstatically up and down on the spot with immense satisfaction.

'Gotcha!' she screamed. Instantly, she regretted it, as her grandfather once again taught her the valuable lesson of maintaining her shield and controlling her emotions, even when you believe yourself to be victorious.

Once their 'computer game' was over, they both sat down, breathing heavily. Primrose had many dark bruises, whereas her grandfather's ghostly form was unmarked, but both were laughing as they re-lived their various moves and techniques.

'You did well, Primrose. No one as young as you has ever managed to hit me, not even Darius. I must be getting old.'

'I understand the inexperience thing now,' she said, leaning against him as he put an arm round her, 'I may have some magic, I might even be good at it... for my age,' she laughed and looked at him, 'but I'm not good at controlling my feelings. I've got a lot to learn.'

'Mastery will come, and I for one am looking forward to training you. Meanwhile, I had better create a fitness programme in order to increase my stamina. You made me work too hard and I am not used to that!'

Primrose felt a little strange, knowing she had just been praised and complimented for real. She quite liked it.

'Primrose,' her grandfather's tone had suddenly turned serious, 'what you want and what you need might not be the same thing. It's taken your grandmother a long time to plan the saving of our family. Even now her plans hang in the balance. My brother is ruthless. Please don't let the saving of the Tree jeopardise the outcome of this long, dreadful 'game', because that is how my brother views this. You can always get a new home and hopefully it will be with us. Trust your grandmother, Primrose. She has all of us in her thoughts and dreams and always will.' Her grandfather paused for a moment and then continued, hugging Primrose closer, 'Some family members though, can never be replaced.'

Her grandfather kissed Primrose's forehead softly.

Primrose realised that her grandfather not only referred to her, but his missing daughter as well.

'Do not let me lose the first granddaughter that dared to hug me and try to kill me on my first day of knowing her… it would break my heart.'

Primrose looked at her grandfather, knowing he spoke honestly with her. She could have cried because of the love she saw in his eyes.

'Don't go all soppy on me, Gramps,' she said with a watery smile, 'I may love you too and I will promise you this: I won't do anything stupid. I think I would like to practise with you too, but next time I won't make allowances for your age!'

Laughing and joking, they made their way back to Elina and Forrestiana.

After many hugs and warnings to remain vigilant, Elina and Primrose used their bracelets to take them back to the Ancient Tree.

On their return, Elina and Primrose were surprised to see how clean the inside of the tree looked; nothing was out of place, despite the damage the explosion should have made. However, as they turned to look at the panel expecting to see a huge hole to their utter astonishment and joy they saw another carving.

Etched into the wood were two girls standing next to each other; one with a single finger touching the centre of a mark; the other alert and waiting, holding a silver net with two proud, young wolves standing close by and ready for action.

Together both girls left the Ancient Tree in search of Dilly and Shadow, each deep within their own thoughts and comforted by each other's presence. It had been a very long day and night, but the new day was still a few hours away. However, neither one of them would sleep until they knew for certain that both Dilly and Shadow were safe and back in their care.

Elina could not wait to see Shadow again, something had begun to worry her. She had a horrible sense of foreboding and it concerned Orion and Ebony, Dilly's parents. She could not understand why they had not come searching for her.

Primrose, though, couldn't believe how lucky she was. She had found some unlikely allies and friends in the past few weeks: a wolf that she had injured badly, a sister she never knew she had and ghosts! Primrose was no longer alone. Her life had had a truly unexpected way of sorting itself out. Primrose knew that she could not take her good fortune for granted; their future was still full of uncertainty, but she felt more than ready to face the danger that threatened them, especially if she had her new friends by her side.

Look out for the third book in the
Battle of the Roses series,

A Show of Force.

Acknowledgements:

Firstly, I would like to thank you, the Reader, for choosing *Unlikely Allies* to read. Seeing my books in other people's hands is quite an emotional experience. It leads to the question of will they or won't they enjoy it, and then to the nervous anticipation for that first review.

I would also like to thank the following people for their support and feedback on my first book and hope that they enjoy *Unlikely Allies* as much as *Primrose*.

A huge thank you to Maddie and the staff at PTS Aylesford for being my first Readers and for the positive feedback they gave me: Karen, Kirsty, Alan, Shaun, Tony, Carol, Luke Kath and Lisa.

To Kirstine Boon, the staff, children and parents of Swingate Primary School for their generosity and a truly magical day - my first book signing!

To my friend, Elaine Chambers, a good friend and ally. Thank you for all of your support and words of encouragement.

A huge thank you to my family and friends for their continued support, which has proved to be invaluable.

To Maria Priestley, who has once again excelled expectations with her design of the front cover and illustrations; to Charlotte

Mouncey for her typesetting skills and completion of the book's jacket. Their skills allow my books to stand out from the rest.

Lastly, my thanks to James Essinger and Amber O'Connor for their constructive advice and The Conrad Press for making another dream come true.